I0450745

A New Life for Emma

Taylor Aspen

Published by Kayler Rose Publishing, LLC, 2025.

This book is dedicated to the hardy pioneers who survived the harsh Nebraska plains.

Chapter 1

F all 1888

Feet aching and shoulders slumped, Emma Cantrell trudged toward her small tenement. It was clear that she was not going to work as a governess in Philadelphia ever again. Her previous boss had made sure of that.

The spiteful Mrs. Buchanon had told everyone she knew, which was pretty much every well-off woman in town, that she had sacked Emma two weeks before for slapping her son.

Emma had not slapped the obnoxious little beggar. The young bully had dumped a bucket of water on her and saturated her with water, and she had given him a stern warning.

The second the words flew out of her mouth, she knew the child would rat on her. What she had not anticipated, though she should have, was his lying about it. She had also not anticipated the harsh punishment his mother had meted out.

Sacked on the spot without even being given the chance to explain what really happened. And because the woman was so upset, she had refused to pay Emma the money she was owed.

Since she had not been able to waste any time, Emma had plunged back into the labor market the following day. She had searched for a job daily ever since, but to no avail.

What am I going to do now? Emma's steps slowed at that thought.

Being a governess was the only thing she knew how to do. She supposed a job at a café or cleaning a boarding house would be a possibility since she could also do those things. She had never used those skills to provide for her livelihood before but that did not mean that she couldn't.

That is if anyone in town will hire me.

Everyone had probably heard about her supposed mistreatment of a child in her care. Between Mrs. Buchanon and all her associates, it was sure to be all over town by now.

Well, if no one in the city will hire me, I can always move to Nebraska. She shuddered at the thought.

Lorette had been begging her to come live on their farm with her and her family for the last couple of years. Emma would only move to Nebraska if she had no other choice left. She had never wanted to move to that God-forsaken place. Her sister seemed to love it there, but Emma had heard too many stories about the plains to want to go there.

The melancholia that was hovering over her today settled in for the duration. She did not want to move to the prairie. She sucked in a deep breath, her lower lip trembling, and tried to summon more optimistic thoughts.

Tomorrow will be better. My luck will change tomorrow. She would pray about it tonight.

Instead of looking for governess work, she would concentrate on cafes, boarding houses, and hotels. That thought improved her mood somewhat, so the rest of the walk home did not seem quite so long.

Resolute, she unlocked the door and stepped inside her cold apartment. She hated living in the tenement, but it was all she could afford on her meager salary. Shutting her front door behind her, Emma picked up her mail from the floor where it had landed when the mailman had slipped it through the slot in her door.

There was a note from the landlord reminding her that rent was due in two days. Sweat beaded on Emma's brow. She would be out on the street if she did not come up with the money by then. Her landlord did not tolerate the rent being late. There were far too many other people the woman could rent the dump to.

Short on the rent after having to use some of the money for it to live off the last two weeks, she had been hoping to make it back. Homeless...she had never been homeless before.

Pushing that thought away she gazed down at the next envelope. It was from Buffalo Springs, but the writing was not her sister's. Instead of Lorette's beautiful flowing penmanship, it was addressed in small, cramped letters. Emma's brow furrowed as she opened it and a train ticket slipped out and fluttered to the floor.

Emma's empty hand flew to her mouth to stifle the gasp that escaped as she read the letter's contents. Her hands shook. *Poor Lorette!* Bending down, she picked up the ticket and gazed at it through tear-filled eyes.

It looked like she would be going to Buffalo Springs after all, but only because of Lorette's poor baby.

The tinny sounds coming from the piano were like an annoying pest Matthew Hoffman wished he could bat off. Sweat beaded his forehead as he tried to focus on the cards in front of him.

It was a good game with money and property at stake, and someone was winning, but he sure wasn't that person. Glancing up at the beer-reddened face of Hustkins, he wondered if it was too late to withdraw his bet.

Of course, it is, you fool.

The snarl from his inner voice came just as Hustkins placed the cards in his hand down on the table with a smug, "Check."

Matthew's stomach clenched. This was the end. As if mocking him, his mind flashed back to a few minutes ago, when he had staked the money without a thought. He had been hoping to out-gamble the mayor. Now, where was he going to get the extra 500 dollars to spare?

"Do you have my money, Hoffman?" The gleam in Hustkins' eyes revealed his anticipation.

Matthew did have the money, but it was to buy more seed for the coming planting season and food for the livestock. He also needed to pay someone to finish cleaning and airing out the big house.

He had planned to do it himself but couldn't bring himself to go back into the house right now. He might never be able to enter it again. The memories would overwhelm him the minute he stepped inside.

Sucking in a deep breath to calm his racing heart, Matthew was only too aware that he had messed up this time. He had never bet that high before and had rarely ever lost a bet, so his confidence had gotten the best of him. He hesitated.

How could he hand over that much cash? He finished off his mug of beer. Maybe there was a chance for him to negotiate his fate a bit. It was worth a try.

As if reading his mind, Hustkins withdrew a pistol from his thick, brown jacket. He was still watching Matthew with an intense stare when he turned the weapon toward him.

The music was like a death march to his ears as Matthew withdrew the money without another hesitation. "That wasn't necessary," he told his drinking buddy with a nod at the gun as he tossed the notes on the table.

"It was," the other man said as he replaced the pistol and scooped up his money.

Matthew pushed back his chair and grabbed his hat.

"You're chickening out?" Hustkins smirked. "You're not even going to try to win your money back?"

Glaring at the man in reply, Matthew strode toward the door, his boots thumping on the creaky wooden floor. He clenched his teeth when the piano player cranked up a happy tune. He stalked out, slamming the door of the saloon on his way.

Outside, he let out a heavy sigh as he trudged through the newly fallen snow to get to the livery stable to pick up his horse. He had taken this same walk several times over the past couple of weeks, but this was the first night he was sober.

Snowflakes fluttered from the gray sky, but the snow would dissipate soon. Winter was coming. He prayed it would be a mild winter so he would not have to buy much feed for the cattle. At least, he had a while to earn the money before the planting season began.

Matthew had looked forward to planting season every year since he was four. That was the year he had first joined his father and brother in the fields. That first year, he had ended up chasing insects and falling asleep under a cottonwood tree. For the first time since that day, he would face planting season alone with no help. He wasn't looking forward to it at all.

That thought alone made Matthew want to head back to the saloon and order two more mugs of beer. But then the memory of the new wooden crosses in the small plot behind the big house would return, and soon he would be buying five more.

Chapter 2

M atthew rode home, still in disbelief over the deaths of his brother and his brother's family. Four of his loved ones, all gone on the same day. They had all fallen ill at the same time. None of them were strong enough to care for the others or to even alert him or the neighbors for help.

His home was on the farm, but it was far away from the big house, so they only saw each other daily during the planting, harvest, and calving seasons. Otherwise, they were each busy with their own tasks.

During slower times, Matthew would take his horse down to share dinner with them three or four days a week. It didn't make him feel any better to remember that he was to have visited them for dinner the day they took ill. Instead, he had postponed the visit until Sunday, three days later, because of a horse he had been trying to sell.

If he had been there, if he had bothered to show up as planned, he would have known they were sick. He would have taken care of all four of them, and none of them would have died. But he had stayed home, instead. He rubbed at a pain in his chest.

Matthew had been shoeing his horse near his stables the morning after his canceled dinner when a neighbor had rushed over. O'Dell had shouted at him to hop on his rattling buggy with him and had raced back to the big house. On the way, he had told Matthew how he had gone over to his brother's house to borrow a plow.

After knocking on the door of the big house for several minutes with no reply, O'Dell had walked around, searching the barn the chicken house, and everywhere else. He had not found anyone but refused to give up since the family wagon was there.

O'Dell had gone back to the house, where the gate to the fence was still hanging open. He had pounded on the door again and then decided to enter. When he walked in, the first thing he had seen was Matthew's brother slumped on the chaise in the front parlor. His face was ashen, and his lips were pale.

Matthew had endured the same sight soon after. He had also had to deal with the sight of the others. The children were the worst. That vision would haunt him for the rest of his life.

He had not felt the same inside since. How could he?

He had to bury them later that same day to avoid any spread in case it was contagious. O'Dell and his wife had helped him lay the four to rest. Matthew had been in disbelief for the rest of the day and even the next.

Everything had hit him on the third day when he had walked into the big house and stood by the door. There had been no fire warming the house. No children screamed his name and ran down to meet him. No one asked him why he was banging about the place as if he owned it. He realized then none of that was ever going to happen again.

That day he broke down. That night he had visited the saloon, something he rarely did. He had drunk himself into a stupor, so the men from the saloon had to load him onto his horse and take him home.

The same men had had to carry him off the next night and the next until people let him alone, alone to drown his sorrow and wallow in his grief.

After that, he had added gambling to his list of sins, when a stumpy man had dared him, and he had accepted the challenge. The game had attracted other fellows who kept the beer flowing and cheered Matthew on. It had been a new high for Matthew, a new high he had indulged in every night since.

Until tonight, he had never bet any large amounts. Now, he had gone and lost a good deal of the farm's capital. Michael would have been so disappointed in him if he were still alive.

Matthew turned the corner that opened to the lonely path that led to his small home, grateful that he was home at last. It was one of the only things Matthew was currently grateful for.

The main thing was Emma.

Emma was his sister-in-law's younger sister. He had never met her, but he was still grateful that she was alive and on her way there. He hoped she might help keep George out of his hair while he worked. It was an inconvenience to haul the baby down to Maddie's farm every morning and pick him back up every night.

The baby...how could he have forgotten about George? He couldn't go home and fall into bed yet.

E mma stood on the wooden boardwalk in front of the Buffalo Springs Depot, tapping her foot. She scanned the dirt street for any sign of a wagon, clenching her hands into fists when she saw no sign of one. *Is the street always this devoid of wagons and people, or is it a special welcome for me?*

Matthew was late. He had told her in his letter that he would meet her at the depot when her train arrived. An hour had passed since then. Everyone else had left long ago.

Emma turned and reentered the building, striding up to the ticket window as fast as her full skirt allowed.

"May I help you, ma'am?" The agent, a short, balding man gave her a welcoming smile.

"My relative was to pick me up. I wonder if you know him...Matthew Hoffman?"

"Of course, I know Mr. Hoffman. Poor man...and you say you're a relative. Well, I must tell you how sorry I am. Poor Mr. Hoffman, suffering a loss like that. Well, I must tell you..."

"Thank you," Emma said before he could go on. "Mr. Hoffman was to pick me up, but he has yet to arrive. I wondered, where is the farm located?"

"The farm...well, it's just a few miles west of here." He indicated the direction with a fling of his arm. "Nice little place. Been in the family for years..."

"Can you tell me how to get there?"

"Of course, of course. You just take the road out of town that heads west. It's about three miles, I'd say. Second farm you come to. But you want to get a wagon at the livery. You can take it out there. The livery is down yonder." He indicated the opposite direction with a fling of his other arm.

"You have been a tremendous help. Thank you. Might I ask for a cup of water?"

"Of course." The man left. He returned seconds later with a cup of water and handed it to Emma."

Emma drank down the cool liquid and returned the cup to the man. "Thank you. I'll be on my way to the livery, then." She made her departure before the man started speaking again.

Outside, Emma gathered her bags from in front of the building. Taking a carryall handle in each hand, she headed toward the livery, her mind in turmoil.

Born and raised in Philadelphia, Emma had never driven a wagon in her life. She had never even driven a carriage or ridden a horse. She hoped there would be a carriage with a driver who could take her to the farm.

No such luck at the livery. As it turned out, there were no carriages in this town besides the few owned by the more well-off families. There was usually a wagon and team to rent, but it was already rented out for the day. As far as someone to drive the wagon, if there had been one, chances were slim on that.

With a sigh, Emma turned from the man and strode back outside, relieved to breathe fresh air and be out of the stench of the livery. There was no help for it. She would have to walk to the farm.

Matthew Hoffman is going to get an earful when I see him! Her brother-in-law was lucky it was a nice day, or he would have to fork out funds for a room at the local hotel for her tonight.

Emma fumed the whole way to the farm, wishing Matthew would come along on his way to pick her up. There was no sign of him. After several rest stops and lugging her baggage for miles, her feet and arms ached, but her temper had not abated. She had passed another farm a short time back. She now wished she had stopped to ask for a ride to Matthew's farm.

Rounding a bend, she spotted a big red barn up ahead. She had already passed one farm, so this must be the one. Beyond the barn was a large white farmhouse. Excitement mingled with sadness to break through some of her anger.

Emma stopped at the edge of the yard to stare up at the large farmhouse her sister had loved so much. Lorette had recorded every milestone of their renovations in letters to her sister. Emma had heard so much about the building but had never laid eyes on it until now. Lorette's excitement about the house had jumped out of the pages in her letters. Seeing it now, Emma understood her sister's enthusiasm.

The house was a simple two-story farmhouse, much like other houses Emma had glimpsed on her way to the farm. The white paint glistened in the pale sunlight. Adorned with white wicker furniture, the porch went around the house as far as she could see. She could picture Lorette's husband, Michael, toiling over each piece as he made them all.

Dried flower stems occupied the beds that surrounded the porch. What Lorette had referred to as the yard turned out to be wind-swept dirt. Stray tufts of dried grass stuck up here and there.

Emma crossed the yard and mounted the front steps. After depositing her bags next to the door, she walked along the porch. As she ran her hand over the porch rail, she admired the hard work that Lorette and Michael had done. She plopped down in one of the chairs, wiping at the tears that came unbidden to her eyes.

The sound of a wagon approaching made her turn to see if Michael's brother had decided to make an appearance. She was still irked he had not bothered to show up at the depot to pick her up when she arrived. Instead, she had had to walk the three miles from town.

A woman pulling a wagon to a halt in the yard squashed Emma's ire but aroused her curiosity. Emma studied the woman's appearance as she descended the porch to meet the woman halfway to the house.

The woman looked older than Emma by a good 10 or more years. Her light brown hair that she had pulled into a bun had streaks of grey showing here and there. There were worry lines around the woman's bright blue eyes. She greeted Emma with a smile.

"Hello, you must be Lorette's sister, Emma. Matthew told me you would be arriving soon." The woman held out a work-worn hand. "I'm Maddie."

Emma accepted Maddie's outstretched hand, noticing how rough it was. *Did Lorette end up with hands like this?* "Hello. It's nice to meet you."

"I saw you walkin' past earlier, but the little ones were down sleepin' so I had to wait till they woke up to come greet ya. Otherwise, I'd a given you a ride the rest of the way. I just live on down the road yonder."

Emma remembered passing the farmhouse about a mile before reaching Lorette's farm.

The other woman turned back to the wagon and lifted down one of the three baskets from the seat. She extended it toward Emma.

Thinking the other woman had brought a basket as a housewarming gift, Emma took it. She peered inside, and to her surprise there was an infant in the basket. She lifted her eyes to Maddie's.

"Matthew's been bringin' George over to my place while he works durin' the day. I thought ya might like to get to know him," Maddie said.

"Oh, George..." Emma sighed when understanding dawned. The one surviving member of Lorette's family. She looked back down at the adorable baby. He gazed up at her with rich brown eyes.

"Hello, George. I'm your Auntie Emma."

"He's eaten, had his afternoon nap, and I changed him. He's all ready to meet ya."

Emma glanced back up at Maddie. "I'm sorry, I don't know where my manners are. Would you like to have a seat on the porch and get acquainted? I haven't been inside the house yet, so I don't know if there is anything to offer you."

Maddie shook her head. "Some other time. I need to get on home and get my work done this afternoon. It has been nice meetin' ya, and I'd love to visit another day."

She pulled another one of the baskets down from the wagon and extended it to Emma. "I brought ya a few things, as well as George's things. I helped Matthew clean out the house. There's not a speck left in the kitchen or pantry. This should get ya by for a day or two."

At a loss for words at the woman's kindness, Emma took the other basket with a nod.

"If ya need anythin' just ride on down to my place. Matthew still has the horses and all are in the barn." Maddie climbed back into the wagon.

"Thank you, Maddie. It was a pleasure meeting you."

Maddie nodded. "I'll be seein' ya."

After Maddie pulled out of the yard, Emma took the two baskets and deposited them onto the porch. She would look through the things Maddie brought later. Right now, she had to get a good look at her nephew. She lifted George out of the basket and held him in her arms.

"Oh, George, you're beautiful..." she whispered as she studied his chubby baby features looking for anything that reminded her of her sister.

The baby smiled at her as if he understood what she had said, and she cuddled him to her, breathing in his fresh, baby smell.

Holding him to her, Emma finished her tour of the yard. As she rounded the corner to the back of the house, she spotted a wide stone well. She was parched again, so she hurried over to it. Upon closer inspection, the well looked as if it had been boarded up. *Why would someone board up the well?*

A gust of wind lifted the strands of hair around Emma's shoulders. It danced about and played with her hair a while before dissipating a bit.

Emma didn't bother trying to smooth her hair. She peered about the yard looking for another well, so she could quench her thirst. Instead of finding another well, her eyes fixed on the four wooden crosses in the small plot beyond the house. All thoughts of a drink of water flew out of her mind.

When the letter had arrived announcing the deaths of Lorette and her family, Emma had tried to make sense of the words it contained but had been unable to.

The full meaning of every sentence and phrase hit her now as she stared at the crosses that Michael's younger brother must have placed on the fresh graves. The small gesture meant a lot to Emma.

But the crosses merely reinforced what the letter had stated. Her older sister was dead. Lorette's husband, Michael, was dead. And their two eldest children were dead.

Emma sniffled. The wind kicked up again as if determined to comfort her and dry her tears. She suspected it should be an old pro at it. It had seen thousands of deaths on this harsh land.

All those deaths were part of the reason Emma had not packed up and moved to join her sister in Nebraska years ago. The stories she had heard about this land from a couple in her tenement building were awful. They had gone West and tried it only to return to Philadelphia after losing everything. They had warned her about the suffering, the toiling, the debts, and then the deaths. All of that had deterred her from coming before.

Lorette's letters had always sounded excited and hopeful, but Emma never bought it. She had heard that most farmers who owned acres and acres of land never really owned that land. They were always in debt. They always needed to take out loans or barter to buy more seed, more livestock, or food for their children. Her neighbors had told her that farmers could work all season but still have every crop die because of insects, the weather, or some other cause. The risks were too high for Emma's comfort.

Now, Emma could see that her fears were justified. The earthy smell of the wild grass, the rough soil under her feet, the stones, the thistle—even the wind—they all combined to enforce nature's power and control. Man was helpless in his quest to conquer and overcome this wild land.

The land had taken away her sister and most of the family she and Michael had worked hard to nurture. All it had taken was a single snap, and it was all gone.

Emma looked down at the family that remained. He was watching her with his big brown eyes. His soft gurgles were barely audible with the sound of the wind.

Looking down at George's soft face, she wondered if he could feel the grief and sadness. Could he tell something had changed? Did he know his real family was gone? Could he feel the sudden loss of those who had cared for him?

She hoped not because she was not sure how to comfort him since they didn't speak the same language yet. George was about nine months old. Emma had no experience with babies. Her charges had always been older children.

"All I can do to comfort you is hold you and love you." Emma placed a kiss on his cheek. "I promise to do everything in my power to take you away from this horrible place and raise you as a proper city boy," she whispered.

George's lips curved into a small grin as if in answer to her statement.

A cough behind Emma caused her to jump. She swirled around to find a strange man standing there. She pulled George to her chest, shielding him with her arms.

Chapter 3

Short black hair curled around the collar of the man's worn tan shirt. The thin material outlined the muscles on his arms and stomach. Brown canvas pants narrowed down to dirt-coated, brown work boots. Deep brown eyes regarded her. The man's expression was stern, angry.

Emma was about to ask him who he was when he introduced himself.

"I am Matthew, Michael's brother..."

Of course, it's just Michael's brother.

The tension eased somewhat from her shoulders. She had heard so much about Matthew from Lorette's letters that she felt almost as if she knew him already even though she had never actually met the man before.

"It's nice to meet you, at last Matthew. I wish it were under different circumstances."

When Matthew grunted, the tension returned to Emma's shoulders.

"Lorette spoke of you often in her letters," she said, trying to build a rapport with him and ease the tension in the air. "She said you owned half the farm."

"I help out...helped out whenever I could..."

"So, you aren't a farmer yourself?"

"I am, but I don't own the main farm. I just worked for Michael."

Emma shook her head, trying to understand. "I thought you inherited part of the farm, same as Michael, split half and half."

"Our father left the farm to both of us, as you say, but Michael bought out most of my share in it. I still own a small piece that I farm for myself. Otherwise, I helped Michael."

"I see. I had no idea. I thought you still owned part of the main farm."

Matthew shrugged. "I'm not sure Lorette knew about it."

"Oh, I thought..."

"It's good of you to come down," Matthew interrupted. "I would give you a tour but that will have to be another time. I need to return to the fields and keep going..."

"It's fine. I can figure it out myself." Emma's voice hardened.

"Great." He turned to leave but hesitated. "Are you sure you'll be okay with George?"

Emma began to assure him that she most certainly would be fine when George pushed himself away from her and stretched his arms out to Matthew. The baby's sudden movement threw her off balance, so she leaned with him, struggling to adjust her hold.

Matthew plucked George from her arms. "Careful."

All Emma could do was stare as Matthew swung the infant to his side. She swallowed and started to reach for George again but let her arms drop to her sides. Matthew looked comfortable with the child, and George looked content. It was obvious Matthew had been a close uncle to the children.

For want of something to do, Emma ran a hand through her hair, trying to smooth out the unruliness. She brushed through the strands with her fingers. She wished she had put it back up after it had fallen out of the pins earlier.

Matthew did not seem to notice her restlessness. He was too engrossed with George. He lifted the boy up until they could look into each other's eyes then he grinned at the boy, his white teeth flashing. George grinned back and giggled.

Resisting the urge to smile at them, Emma swung her gaze away. It settled once again on the graves. "George never took the fever?"

"No. He hasn't shown any sign of it at all. The doc claims he is in the clear."

"Do you know what caused the sickness?" Emma turned back to Matthew.

"Doc thinks the well water is bad. That's why I boarded it up." He indicated the well she had noticed earlier. "He says that's why George didn't get it since he was still...he was still at his mother's breasts," he said in a rush.

Something about the way Matthew said that last phrase caused Emma's cheeks to heat. Ignoring her warm face, she said, "So, some bad water? That's what took my sister's life?"

Busy making silly faces at George, Matthew turned to look at her. "That's one possibility. It could have been a fever of some kind. Doc said something about how George's mother's milk protected him from contracting it. No one else around has gotten sick..."

"And I didn't even get a chance to say goodbye. I wish I could have at least been here for the funerals."

"That would have been nice...if there had been any." Matthew hugged George to him. "I had to bury their bodies right away to keep others from contracting the illness, in case that is what it was."

"No funeral at all?" Emma's stomach twisted at the thought.

"No, no funeral at all," Matthew said.

With tears welling in her eyes, Emma fell silent.

"Look, I really need to return to..."

"Do you mind if I have a moment alone?" Her voice was hoarse with unshed tears.

"Of course." He held George toward her but pulled him back with a frown when she made no effort to take him. "I really need to get back..."

A strangled sob escaped Emma's throat and a line of tears raced down her cheeks.

"George and I will be waiting for you in front." Matthew sighed and walked away.

When the sound of his footsteps faded away, Emma sank to her knees with a long wail. The gravity of her loss twisted her stomach in cramps, causing her to cry harder. It was as if her heart were being ripped out and torn to shreds.

Her hope had been that she would arrive here to find that it was all a big mistake. But it was real. Her sister was gone.

Once she cried herself out, Emma stood and composed herself before going in search of the menfolk. She found Matthew seated on the front porch steps with George on his lap. He was tickling the infant who squirmed and squealed in delight.

Matthew laughed in response to George's antics. It was a hearty laugh drawn from deep within his chest—the laugh of someone who did not do it often enough.

Emma could not hold back a smile as she watched them frolic. It was nice to see Matthew trying to fill George's life this way after the loss the infant had suffered.

At last, she let out a sigh and trudged over to where they sat. Matthew looked up at her and sprang to his feet.

"I'm sorry I took a while," Emma said, her voice soft.

"I understand." Matthew's voice hardened and his smile disappeared making it appear that he did not understand at all.

George let out a yawn and buried his head in Matthew's shoulder.

Puzzled by Matthew's gruffness, Emma said, "I'll take him now." Her attempt to take George into her arms was met with resistance from the boy. She took one of his small, soft hands in hers and tried to coax him to come to her, but he stuck to his uncle.

"Come on, bud. I need to head back to work." Matthew tried to urge George, but the infant let out a stubborn wail in response.

It took some enticing, but Emma won out after fishing a cookie out of the pocket of her dress. George went to her willingly and took the proffered treat. Emma laughed as she straddled George on her hip while he gnawed on the cookie.

"And that's how we do it in the city," Emma said superiorly, looking down her nose at Matthew.

"We should not encourage that," Matthew said as he turned and stalked off.

Oblivious to the slobber that ran down her arm from George, Emma shot a dark look after Matthew's retreating back. *What is the matter with him?*

Matthew said he had cleaned and aired out the house, but Emma could not help being wary as she took a careful step inside. Afterall, some unknown fever had wiped out four people she loved in a matter of hours.

As she wandered through the house, she assessed it, gauging it by what Lorette had told her. The inside was more beautiful than her sister had described. Michael had made all the furniture, which was stunning. The wood glowed with a fine shine. The quilt and decorative items showed Lorette's fine hand with a needle and thread. The whole house had a warm and cozy feel to it, a place one could curl up in and sleep for days.

Emma smiled. She could picture her sister living here. The house and everything inside it screamed Lorette. It was a place that Emma had always dreamed of having for herself someday, her own space that she could decorate according to her own taste and heart's desire.

In Philadelphia, she had bunked in a small room that she paid for monthly. It had been dingy, and she had not been allowed to change a thing. She had not been allowed to even hang her needlework on the walls.

Several weeks had elapsed since the deaths and Matthew's cleaning job. A fine layer of dust already covered the inside of the house.

Matthew had not picked her up from the depot, nor had he bothered to carry in her bags. Emma was steaming as she collected her things and the baskets that Maddie had brought. After searching through the baskets, she found some milk for George and plenty of food to fix a few meals. There were even cleaning supplies as well. *Bless you, Maddie. You thought of everything.*

Once Emma scrubbed the kitchen, she fed George and made him a bed of blankets on the floor in the corner of the front room. He was asleep almost as soon as he laid his head down. Emma stood staring at his chubby face as he slept, wondering how on earth she was going to care for him.

"**A**nd to think I was excited for her to arrive," Matthew muttered to himself as he stalked back to the field. He had been looking forward to someone to help with George but also someone to grieve with.

The second he had come up behind her, she had jumped like a frightened rabbit. And the way she held George to her, the wary look in her eyes, he had known her type.

She was one of those people, the type who thought that because they lived in the city, they had it better than those out in the country. They approached everything related to the country and farms with suspicion, as if anything and everything was out there to harm them.

Who would even want to touch such a scrawny figure?

It was true that Emma was as beautiful as Lorette had been. Maybe even more so as her beauty was younger and spicier. Still, Matthew could not help the unkind thought. He hated anyone who looked down on the place he called home.

He hated it when people, who knew nothing about how the land worked, acted as if they knew all about it. They thought they could even predict outcomes. And he especially hated it when city people who took no risks in life acted like they were some special breed of people.

Well, he had had enough of them.

His aunt had been one. All the woman did was whine and whine to his uncle until he had died. She had whined about how much they could have accumulated if they had gone back to live in the city they had come from.

Then, he himself had the intense misfortune of falling in love with another whining woman. He agreed that everyone deserved to pursue life the way they wanted to. He did not agree that that gave them the right to look down on others.

Hannah had laughed when she realized he was not joking, that he seriously wanted to homestead and build a family there on the farm and to farm the land for the rest of his life. Farming was in his blood. He was born and raised on the farm and had no intention of giving it up.

They met when he was on a trip to Chicago and fell instantly in love. The brief, whirlwind romance had ended with them married. Before taking her back home to the farm, Matthew had spent his whole savings taking her on a honeymoon to New York City. The two of them had been so much in love then, or so he thought.

When he brought her home and showed her the farm, her switch from dizzying love to obvious blatant disgust had been quick. It had cut him deep and convinced him it had all been a façade. He could understand her not wanting this life, but he could not understand her instant hatred of him because he did. She had headed straight back to Chicago, leaving him with a broken heart and a bitterness toward women.

There was no understanding it. In his eyes, homesteading was beautiful. It came with a lot of sorrow, as well as joy, but pretty much everything in life did. People still contracted diseases and died in the city. You could starve in the city. You could lose your home in an instant in the city. Everything that could happen in the country could happen anywhere else.

Lorette had understood that and embraced life here. He wondered how she and Emma could have been sisters. All he knew was that he was not going to let Emma come down here and cause him frustration. He was already knee-deep in grief and worry as it was.

Matthew walked the field he had plowed earlier in the day and tossed out the large rocks the plow had unearthed. He had planned to plant a new crop or two next year and was preparing the field to winter over.

As he worked, he wondered if he was even doing the right thing in letting Emma stay alone with George. Parenting or even looking after a child was hard work. It was not something a person could choose to take a break from because she felt like it.

According to Lorette, Emma worked as a governess in Philadelphia. That was the only reason he had decided to trust her with George. She had a fair amount of experience with kids. The two of them would survive the next few hours until he returned...he hoped.

Frustrated, Matthew slung a rock out of his way with a growl. He had been looking forward to some sort of company, someone to plan out George's future with. Instead, like other recent days, he couldn't wait to finish his work and trudge back to the saloon.

Once he finished working for the day, Matthew still wanted to head to the saloon but decided he better head to the main house instead. He needed to check on George and make sure he was doing okay in Emma's care. He was not anxious to encounter Emma again, however, so to put it off longer he went to his house to wash up.

If she decided to stay in the big house, he would need to dig another well. He didn't think she would stay, though. In the meantime, he would haul a barrel of water over for her to use. After he finished washing his hands and face, he slicked back his wet hair with his hands. Then he set to work loading a barrel into the back of his wagon.

Once he had filled the barrel with water from his well, Matthew could find no other excuse to delay the inevitable any longer. Apprehension churning in his gut, he headed the team toward the big house. He was not looking forward to another brush with Emma and her snooty attitude, but he was not about leave George in her care overnight. He would be taking the infant back home with him tonight.

To keep as much water as he could from sloshing over the side of the barrel, Matthew took it slow. He did not mind that it was taking longer tonight to make the trip. After meeting Emma, he wished he had never invited her to come out. He shook himself for the selfish thought. She just lost her sister, as he had lost his brother. He had had the idea that they would form a bond due to George and the bond would be stronger due to the mutual losses they shared.

"Hmph," he snorted. So much for that idea. The first time they met each other it was hate at first sight for them both. For some reason, she brought out the worst in him. Why couldn't she be more like Lorette? He had admired and respected Lorette. She had been a strong woman eager to take on new challenges.

His hope was to find someone like her someday. If he was honest with himself, he would admit that he had had a small inkling that maybe Emma would be the one for him. He had thought for sure that she would be like Lorette. Instead, she had turned out to be a snooty city woman, the exact opposite of what he wanted in a wife.

It was hard to even be polite to her. He determined to try his best as he stopped the wagon in front of the big house and jumped down. The soft glow of a lantern shone through the front window and an appetizing aroma drifted out to him. Sucking in a deep breath, he released it as he entered the house.

Walking inside, the first thing he noticed was the shine on the wooden floors. They had not glowed like that in a long time. Lorette had been an excellent housekeeper, but three young children took a lot of work. This had prevented her from keeping the floors glowing like she had before their births.

Matthew followed the enticing scents to the dining table, his mouth watering. A feast was all laid out and his determination to be nice to Emma crashed to the ground. Where had she gotten the food to cook and the cleaning supplies? He had cleaned everything out of the house as a necessary precaution in case the deaths were due to something contagious.

Emma had not sought him out in the field to get the supplies from him, so where did she get her hands on all the food that he now saw covering the table? There was also a quart jar of milk. *Did she go shopping in town before coming out here when we have everything we need right here on the farm?*

His temper flared at her wasteful use of money. She may have plenty of it herself, he had no idea, but if she planned to stay here, she would need to learn that money was not easy to come by on the farm.

Out here, you had to stretch it to the fullest. You had to make it last throughout the year until the next year's harvest got sold. And sometimes that did not work out the way you planned it to, so you had to have some tucked away for emergencies. You could not go spending it on items raised right here on the farm.

Emma happened to pop out of the kitchen at that moment. "Oh good, it is you..." She stuttered to a stop when she raised her eyes to his face.

Matthew noted that her face turned pale as she stumbled back a step, but he unleashed the full force of his hangover, and anger with himself on her anyway.

Chapter 4

Matthew's sudden tirade left Emma speechless.

"What is the meaning of this? Where did all this food come from? Did you *actually* go shopping in town for all this? We have everything you could possibly need here on the farm. You had to just come let me know and I would have gotten it for you."

Emma managed to find her voice just as Matthew paused for a breath. "I beg your pardon, but I worked myself ragged this afternoon cleaning this place and fixing you a good meal." She indicated the steaming chicken pot pie she had placed on the table along with green beans, applesauce, fresh hot rolls, and a pie that was cooling on the sideboard for dessert.

She held up a hand when Matthew started to speak. "Don't you say another word. It's my turn to speak. How dare you berate me like a child? And how dare you question how I did any of this?

You have been nothing but rude to me since you met me this afternoon. You should be apologizing to me and thanking me for the meal, not shouting at me. And, for your information, your wonderful neighbor brought me a basketful of supplies when she dropped George off this afternoon."

Anger dropping from his face like a mask, Matthew attempted to speak again, but Emma continued. "Which, by the way, she stopped over when she saw me pass by her farm on my way here...when I walked all the way from town to the farm because there was no one at the depot to pick me up when I arrived!" Emma's voice had risen with every word until she was fairly screaming.

Matthew's face flushed scarlet. "I...," he began, but George chose that moment to let out a wail.

"Now look what you've done. All this yelling has upset the baby." Emma tossed Matthew a glare as she hurried to George and scooped him up. "I think it's best if you leave."

"It's alright, Georgie," Emma soothed as she turned her back on Matthew. She pulled the baby close and rocked him to calm him, as well as herself.

At the sound of the front door closing, she turned around to look where her brother-in-law had been standing. "The gall of the man!" she said to George who had quit crying the moment the door shut.

After feeding George, Emma tried to eat but she couldn't enjoy the meal she had been looking forward to. She pushed the food around on her plate a few more times before giving up with a sigh. She put the food in the pie safe for the night and cleaned the kitchen. When she was finished, she put George to bed before retiring herself.

Tired as she was, she found sleep elusive. Her thoughts and emotions were all in a jumble after everything that had happened that day. She didn't understand it. Lorette had always spoken so highly of Matthew in her letters. Emma did not find him agreeable at all. She could not fathom why her sister had liked him so well.

Oh, well, maybe it was for the best. She and Matthew didn't need to get along anyway since her plan was to take George and return to Philadelphia. Emma shivered. If Matthew could get so upset over a meal she had cooked, then she didn't want to even imagine his reaction when she told him her plans.

For now, she would hold off on telling him, and try to get along with him. Snuggled under the colorful quilt Lorette had made, Emma dozed off.

M atthew closed the door behind him and released a breath.

Well, now, he had gone and done it. He shouldn't have said anything about the meal she had fixed, other than 'thank you'. When would he learn to keep his mouth closed?

Of course, Maddie had brought the food when she had brought George over. He was too rattled over his poker losses the previous night to realize that George had to have gotten there with Emma somehow.

To make matters worse, *he* had forgotten to pick her up from the depot, so she had walked the three miles from town to the farm.

What a cad she must think him. He hesitated outside the front door, feeling guilty and confused. He should go back in and apologize but was afraid of the reception he would get if he tried.

Best to give her some time to cool off. He would apologize in the morning and set things right. Women were complicated. He never knew how to handle them.

At last, Matthew unhitched the wagon to leave the barrel of water he had forgotten to tell her about and take care of the team. He left the horses in the barn there. After he gathered wood from the pile he and his brother had split, he left a stack on the covered front porch. He walked toward home.

As he stepped inside his small house, his stomach grumbled, reminding him that he had ruined the evening before he had gotten to sample that delicious-smelling meal. All he had in the larder was a couple of biscuits and some bacon left over from breakfast. The thought was unappetizing, but his stomach insisted that he feed it, so he ate what was left and trudged off to bed.

While he lay awake staring into the darkness, he realized he should have gone over to the saloon, instead, but somehow, the thought did not appeal to him like it had on previous nights. He knew that even with his exhaustion, it would be some time before he could get himself to sleep. Yet, he still didn't feel like drowning in alcohol tonight.

Maybe it had something to do with the arrival of Emma. More likely, it had something to do with the amount of money he had lost the previous night. That was probably also the reason he had lost his temper with Emma over what he thought had been wasteful spending of money.

What a hypocrite he was, getting on her about money when he had gambled his away. Guilt assailed him once again. Great, now he was being rude to others because of his own failings. He had hit a new rock bottom.

T he next morning, Matthew awoke early and got dressed. Sleep had been elusive due to his guilty conscience. He needed to make things up to Emma, but he was unsure how to go about it. He thought long and hard about it while he cared for the animals.

Once the animals were cared for, the eggs gathered, and he had a fresh bucket of milk to deliver to Emma, he headed to the big house. Still, he had no idea what to do to make it up to Emma, but he was sure something would come to him.

Sitting the bucket of milk down, Matthew paused at the door to the house. He sure hoped she had cooled down during the night. He didn't relish starting his day with a chewing out.

Sucking in a deep breath, he let it out slowly and then rapped on the door. There were footsteps and then Emma pulled the door open.

"I wasn't sure if you'd come over for breakfast or not." Emma greeted him.

Holding out his hat full of fresh eggs in one hand, he lifted the bucket of milk. "I brought a peace offering. I apologize for my behavior last evening. I was way out of line."

A slight smile curved her lips. "Come in. I'll finish making breakfast."

Relieved Emma was not going to be difficult about the previous night, Matthew stepped inside. The aroma of frying ham hit him, and his stomach let out an appreciative grumble.

After finishing a delicious breakfast, Matthew entertained George while Emma cleaned up the kitchen.

As she dried the dishes, Emma wondered why Matthew was still hanging around instead of heading out to work. She found out as she dried the last plate and placed it in the cupboard.

"I am here to give you a tour," Matthew said.

"A tour?"

"Yes." He nodded. "You need to see the farm and, well, it's my job as a host to show it to you and explain a few things about it."

"Oh, you don't have to bother..."

"I do," Matthew said matter-of-factly. "I am sorry about all I said last night, it was wrong of me. Please allow me to make it up."

Emma realized Matthew was a man of few words. He was also a man who didn't bother with beating about the bush or fancy speech. He just attacked issues head-on. Emma could live with that...at least for the time that they had to see each other.

"Well, I'll go get a bonnet and shawl then."

Matthew smiled. "Great. I'll get George ready." He dashed off with George in his arms.

Emma smiled at his enthusiasm and then went to don her bonnet and shawl.

Matthew helped Emma and George into the wagon, and they set off. The farm was huge, stretching out acre after acre. The land was mostly empty fields, plowed up to winter over.

Emma gasped at the wide expanse. "Michael owned all of this?"

"Most of the time." Matthew shrugged. "Sometimes he needed to take out a loan to get by, so he used the land as collateral."

Emma thought he was joking. When she realized he wasn't, she gaped at him. "But if he doesn't pay up..."

"They take the land, yes. That's why I said most of the time. But Michael was a good and industrious worker. He only lost a part of his land once—that was to Maddie's father-in-law—but he never lost any land again. He always paid up on time after that."

"Why didn't he just rely on his capital for planting?"

"He could have." Matthew shrugged. "But then he wouldn't be ready for emergency expenses when they came knocking and he wouldn't be able to plant as many crops as he would have wanted."

Emma shook her head. She did not understand it, but it did sound interesting. She imagined living like that, on your toes all year long. No wonder Lorette always sounded so excited.

"Didn't he have any farm hands?" she asked.

Matthew nodded. "He did but they always went to their real homes after harvest and returned in spring for the planting season. I supervised the crew."

George let out a wail to let them know he wanted more attention. Matthew looked down at him on Emma's lap and smiled.

At that moment, Emma realized the picture they painted with Matthew driving the wagon and her carrying George on her lap beside him. It was a picture her sister and Michael must have painted many times before.

Matthew said he had just wanted to show her around, show her the whole layout of the farm. That way she knew where the chicken coop was, where the cow's stall was, and even where Michael's horses were. By the time they got to the chicken coop, he insisted she gather the eggs.

"What? I don't know how to gather the eggs. You will need to teach me how."

Matthew chuckled. "Gathering eggs is not a skill someone learns. It is not something hard to do. You just gather the eggs.

Crossing her arms, Emma said, "I will not gather them unless you show me how."

Chuckling again, Matthew demonstrated twice for her but gave in when she insisted that he show her a third time.

Still, when she handed George over and made her first attempt, she gathered up her gown and ran out of the coop within minutes of entering.

Matthew burst into laughter, and George squealed along with him, adding to Emma's consternation.

"You are the human. They should be running, not you, Emma," he said between chuckles.

"They don't know that," she said in defense.

"Try again."

"What? No!"

"Come on."

Aiming Matthew her dirtiest look, she stomped into the pen. She made it to the middle of the room before squirming in fright. "They are coming closer. Why are they coming closer?" Her voice rose to a high pitch, but she didn't care.

"Relax. They just think you have food."

"They think I am the food!" Emma screeched as she ran out of the coop once again.

Slapping his hands on his thighs, Matthew doubled over in laughter. George clapped his hands excitedly. By the time he looked up, Emma was standing in front of him with her hands on her hips.

"Don't do that."

"I'm sorry, I don't mean to laugh. It's just I haven't seen anything this funny in a long time." Matthew apologized, but a grin still softened his face. "Try again."

With a groan, Emma waded in again.

"Don't stop," Matthew prodded from the sidelines when she hesitated.

Emma looked up at him as he drew George's hand away from a nail the child was trying to grab and shifted closer to the door.

"Oh my..." she said as she just missed stepping in chicken droppings.

"Don't look down and don't stop. Just keep going till you reach the eggs."

Wiping her sweaty palms on her apron, Emma followed his instructions.

"Come on. You're almost there."

Stepping carefully, she walked on, looking into the air and not at her feet. With a sigh, she reached the nests.

"Good. Now, pick up one of those baskets and fill it."

"They will attack me with their beaks," Emma squawked, as she lowered her hand toward the nest.

"I know, but it doesn't hurt," Matthew said.

Emma sprang up again causing him to burst into another round of laughter.

"I'm kidding," he said.

Emma let out a sigh.

"Come on, the eggs." Matthew dived back to business.

"Anyone ever told you that you are like a pushy taskmaster?" Emma asked.

"A lot of people have," he said with another chuckle. "Fill up the basket and come back to us."

Emma giggled despite her nervousness.

"The eggs won't bite, just pick them up with purpose."

Sucking in a deep breath Emma reached into the nest and grabbed hold of the egg.

"Good. Now gather the eggs from the rest of the nests and then come out but try not to drop the basket."

Another sigh escaped Emma as she did as he instructed, then turned and waddled out of the coop again.

"You did it!" Matthew clapped and George joined in, clapping his hands with enthusiasm and giggles.

A rush of pride hit Emma. She had overcome her fear of the chickens and successfully gathered the eggs. Surprised at the feeling of accomplishment and the excitement that shot through her, she climbed onto the wagon with Matthew's help. She set the basket on the floor in front of her and with a smile took George from Matthew's outstretched hands.

When they reached the big barn where the cows were housed, Matthew brought the wagon to a halt.

"Oh, no..." Emma whispered.

"Come on. This will be just as fun," he said.

"Yes, for you," Emma countered.

Matthew snickered and got off the wagon, reaching up for her and George.

Once in the barn, Emma stood by the door of the stall and watched Matthew milk the cow like an old pro, which she supposed he was since he had been raised on the farm.

"Just know that applying the right amount of pressure to the right spot will allow the milk to come gushing out."

The man made it seem so easy, but it was not. At Emma's first attempt, she squirmed so much that the cow sensed her fear and became restless.

"You need to relax. The cow trusts you with this. If you are not relaxed, she will think you're going to hurt her."

"Are you serious? Does it really think all that?" Emma stared down at the creature that had quieted down suddenly.

With a grin, Matthew shrugged. "That was what our mother always said and I'm sticking to it. Animals can sense your fear, and that makes them nervous."

Emma rolled her eyes and settled on the small stool again. This time she managed to stay calm but try as she could, the milk only came out in small trickles.

"You have to apply more pressure," Matthew said.

She applied more pressure, groaning from the pain and effort.

She did better on her fourth attempt. The milk gushed out and into the bucket as it had for Matthew. Emma squealed in delight despite the pain her hands were in. When she was finished milking, Matthew let the stock out into the pasture.

By the time they got back to the house, it was almost time for the midday meal, so Emma rushed inside to prepare food.

After taking care of the horses and wagon, Matthew took the basket of eggs into the house and set it on the table. "I'll take the milk out to the spring house to store it and churn some butter from some of the cream."

Busy scrambling an egg for George, Emma nodded.

By the time Matthew returned with a fresh batch of butter, Emma had fed George and laid him down for a nap. She dished up the scrambled eggs and set a basket of biscuits on the table.

"Are those biscuits?" Matthew looked surprised.

Emma smiled. "Special recipe. I hope that butter is well churned because you are going to need something of high quality for those biscuits."

Matthew smiled and licked his lips. "Can't wait."

They took their seats and dug in.

Emma glanced up from her meal at intervals to gauge if he was enjoying it, but Matthew was eating quietly.

When he was finished eating, Matthew sat back in his chair.

"Those biscuits are delicious. I don't think I have ever eaten such fluffy biscuits." He smiled, revealing a dimple Emma hadn't noticed before. Enchanted, she couldn't pull her eyes away.

"What?" he asked when she continued to stare at him.

Focused on those charming dimples, it took a minute for Emma to respond. "Do you mean that?"

Leaning toward her, he said, "The biscuits are amazing, Emma."

"Thank you," she said, dropping her face before he could see the blush that was sure to be spreading across her cheeks.

But it was too late. "Are you blushing?" Surprise tinged his voice.

"No." she denied, but he reached over with a hand and tilted her head back up, bursting out laughing. "You are blushing."

Emma rolled her eyes and shook her face free. "Didn't you mention you have some work to do around the farm this afternoon? You better stop dawdling and get to it."

Matthew laughed again but did not argue.

Chapter 5

The next day was spent much as the previous one. Matthew came by for breakfast. After eating, they were all outside so that Emma could receive more lessons around the farm.

When they reached the barn, Matthew brought his horse out of his stall and led him over to Emma. "Emma, this is Storm."

He showed Emma how to put a halter, bit, and bridle on his horse. He then showed her how to remove them. After several demonstrations, he took George from her and stood back to watch her try.

Emma eyed the horse dubiously. He was large and black, and his size was intimidating. She talked to the animal and stroked his head and face as Matthew had done. When the horse was used to her, she attempted to put the halter on the horse, but he pulled away every time she tried. It took several tries before she finally managed to get it all on the horse.

"Next, you learn how to saddle the horse," Matthew said. He demonstrated how to put the blanket on first, then the saddle. He then showed her how to cinch it down under the horse's belly. Once he was finished with several repeats of the steps, Matthew again took George from her and stood aside.

"That looks simple enough," Emma said as she moved forward to put the blanket on the horse's back. When it came to the saddle, though, it was a different story. She struggled to lift the heavy saddle up high enough to get it onto the horse.

After several attempts, she stood aside and looked over at her instructor.

"Is this really necessary? I don't even know how to ride a horse, so I don't see why I need to know how to do any of this."

"We live on a farm, Emma. You need to learn to ride a horse, but first, you need to know how to saddle one and ready him to ride. After lunch, you learn how to ride him," Matthew patiently explained.

Emma pouted some more before she gave in and tried again. She would prove to Matthew that she could do this or she'd die trying. It took three more tries before she was able to heft the saddle onto the horse's back and attempted to cinch down the straps.

She stepped back and smiled at Matthew. "There, I did it!"

"Good job," Matthew said as he approached the horse. He grabbed the loose straps and cinched them tighter. "You have to be sure the saddle is cinched down tight, or it will do you no good. You'll start riding and you and the saddle will slide off and hit the ground."

The smile slipped from Emma's face and she stuck her tongue out at Matthew's back while he finished checking the straps.

Stepping away from the horse, he looked at Emma. "Now you need to get it back off of the horse."

"Why? You said I'm learning how to ride. Can't we do it now instead of after lunch?"

"No, first you need to learn how to saddle and unsaddle the horse properly. You can attempt riding after lunch."

With an exasperated sigh, Emma returned to the horse's side and reversed the previous process. Once she had the straps undone, the saddle slid off easily, almost knocking Emma to the ground with its weight.

Matthew insisted she repeat the procedure over and over again before he was satisfied and finally quit for lunch.

After a quick lunch of meat and cheese wrapped in bread, Matthew led Emma back outside to the barn.

"Are you ready for a ride?" he asked as they entered the barn.

"As ready as I'll ever be, I suppose," Emma said, her voice tinged with fear.

"You'll be fine." Matthew led her to the tack room. "Grab your saddle and gear and bring everything out to the stalls." He turned, leaving her to do as he asked. He returned to the stall area.

After a few minutes, Emma joined him, her gear in tow.

"I don't know how I'm ever going to mount that giant horse you have, let alone ride it." She indicated Matthew's horse he used to teach her to saddle with.

"I had hoped you would be more excited for your riding lesson," he said dryly. "That giant as you called him is my horse, so you won't be riding him. You'll ride Buttercup." He indicated the beautiful Palomino in the stall behind him. "She's a gentle horse and smaller than Storm. You should do just fine with her."

Emma stamped her foot. "Why did you teach me to saddle that giant if I'm going to be riding a smaller horse?"

Matthew couldn't help grinning at her temper tantrum. "Now settle down. You don't want to upset the horses," he said soothingly. "I used my horse so that if anything were to happen to me and my horse was the only one around, you would be able to handle saddling him."

"Well then I should learn how to ride the beast if I might have to do it someday," Emma said with a stubborn tilt to her head.

"You will, just not your first time. Once you get used to riding Buttercup, you'll get a turn on Storm." He turned his back on her as he readied George in a small wagon Michael had made for the kids, so Lorette could take the wee ones for a walk with her. "Now, go saddle your horse, Emma."

When Matthew had George settled in his wagon and turned back toward Buttercup's stall, he was happy to see Emma saddling the horse.

Once Emma had her mount ready, he showed her how to mount the horse. It took Emma several tries, but she finally made it.

He led Emma and her horse out of the barn into the pasture, giving Emma instructions as he walked.

Emma caught onto riding as if she had been born doing it, surprising Matthew with her performance.

"Are you sure you haven't ridden before?" he said half in jest, half seriously.

"No, this is my first time. I guess I have a natural knack for it."

"Well, then we'll need to go for a proper ride. Wait here while I saddle Storm. We'll ride around the meadow together and later in the week, we'll have a proper ride."

Matthew hurried back into the barn where he readied his mount, then grabbed George out of his wagon and mounted his horse, holding George in front of him.

"Is that safe to ride with George like that?" Emma asked when he joined her in the pasture.

"George and I are riding buddies. There have been several times I've had to take him out with me when I've gone out to ride the fences and such. He loves it. Don't you, George?"

George giggled and clapped in joy.

"I guess you know what you're doing then," Emma said.

They spent the next few hours riding around the meadow before Matthew called it a day with Emma's lessons. George was getting fussy and fighting sleep. "George needs to go in for a nap. I'm impressed with your progress today, Emma. We'll have more lessons tomorrow."

Emma sighed as she followed Matthew back to the barn.

That evening after Matthew left, Emma groaned in pain as she climbed into bed. She wasn't used to doing everything she had done the last two days, and her body let her know it wasn't happy with her. She ached in places she never thought could get sore.

Matthew had assured her that she would get used to riding and it would be easier each time until she wouldn't be sore anymore after a ride, but right now she was dubious about that.

The next day, Matthew taught Emma how to harness the team of horses and hook them up to the wagon. As the previous day, he made her practice over and over again until he was satisfied with her performance. After lunch, he had her hitch the team to the wagon, and he taught her how to drive the wagon.

Emma struggled with learning to drive the wagon, not taking to it like she had riding a horse. It frustrated her. She thought surely it would be as easy as riding was to her and was disappointed when it wasn't.

She finally got the hang of it by the end of the afternoon when Matthew called it a day, so George could take a nap.

The next few days were spent riding over the rest of the property with Matthew, and then with Emma driving the wagon down the road a short way.

Emma was sore and tired by the time Matthew said they were finished with her lessons, but she was glad he had taught her all that he had. Her new knowledge and skills made her feel empowered.

Chapter 6

"I have a surprise for you," Matthew said after breakfast a week later. The two of them had fallen into a routine after the tour of the farm. Matthew's respect for Emma had continued to grow. Matthew realized he actually liked Emma and was even starting to admire her. The attraction he felt for her hit him hard. There was no way they could be right for each other.

Emma's brow quirked at him. "A surprise?" She looked as shocked as he felt.

He couldn't stop a grin from spreading across his face. "We're taking a trip into town today."

"We are? To town?" She frowned. "What for? I thought you said we went into town on Saturday afternoons and we both have work that needs to be done around here today."

"I need a few supplies and the pantry needs to be restocked. Plus, it will be a nice break." He grinned. "It looks to be a warm day today."

The look Emma gave him was still dubious.

"Come on, I'll take you on a tour of the town, and after we get our supplies, I'll treat you two to lunch at the hotel."

It was as if sunshine lit the room when Emma smiled. "Just let me freshen up and get George ready." She untied her apron and tossed it onto the table before scooping George from his seat. "Did you hear that, Georgie? We're going to town."

"Great. I'll go hitch the team to the wagon and you two can meet me outside." Matthew practically ran out the door, not sure why he was so excited that Emma had agreed to go with him today.

Once they were all in the wagon, Matthew covered Emma and George with a rug before clucking to the team.

Emma chattered away with George, responding to his sporadic bursts of gurgles as though they carried on a two-sided conversation.

Matthew had lost the thread of what Emma was saying a few miles back, but a strange peacefulness settled over him while he listened to her and his small nephew acting as though they understood each other.

He slowed down as they neared town and pointed out things they passed along the way. He waited for her to mention that she had seen some of those things on her long walk to the farm, but she didn't. Maybe she had forgiven him his unintended slight.

Once the tour ended, Matthew dropped Emma and George off at the General Store. "I need to run over to the lumber mill and get some wood. You pick out what you need here, and I'll pay for it when I come back to pick you both up." He waited until Emma nodded at him and then he hopped back into the wagon, whistling as he headed down the block.

When Matthew pulled up in front of the lumber mill, several men were deep in conversation.

"Hey Matthew," the men called to him.

Matthew nodded at them as he clambered down from the wagon.

"How're things going out at the farm with that new housekeeper of yours?" Jake Ballinger asked with a grin that looked suspiciously like a leer.

"She's my sister-in-law, not my housekeeper. She's here to help with George," Matthew said. "But things are going fine, just fine."

"How's George doing? He settlin' in okay with the gal?" Luke Swallow joined in.

"They're doin' fine, getting' along real well."

"I saw the gal when she first came into town. She's quite a looker, like her sister." Jake said.

"I guess so," Matthew said in a terse voice. There was something about Ballinger that always irritated him. For some reason, his irritation doubled when the man mentioned Emma.

"I hear ya lost a load of money a while back to the Mayor." Jake slugged him in the arm, laughing.

Gnashing his teeth together, Matthew nodded in reply.

"When ya gonna play again, I want a shot at ya." Ballinger laughed again.

Ignoring the annoying man, Matthew approached the mill owner and put in his order. "I'll pick it up on Saturday," he finished, not wanting to hang around there any longer than necessary. Ballinger had already killed his good mood.

After Matthew left, Emma placed her pantry order with the store owner's wife, Mrs. McBurney. The two women chatted for a few minutes before the older woman left to gather the requested items. Emma strolled to the fabric area and browsed the bolts, looking for the right choices.

She wanted to make Matthew a new Sunday shirt for church, since she had noticed the cuffs were fraying on his old one. George had outgrown his Sunday outfit, so she would need fabric for George a new outfit, too. The variety of material for such a small frontier town surprised Emma.

After the grocery order was ready, Mrs. McBurney came back to cut the required amount of each fabric. Emma shifted George to her left side as she scanned the thread and buttons. George liked the shiny brass buttons and tried to grab some out of the basket. Emma turned to keep George from getting at the buttons and chose the ones he liked for his outfit.

Emma was holding a spool of thread up to the teal-colored fabric she had picked for Matthew's shirt. A man sidled up next to her, his eyes scanning her face. They worked their way down to her feet as he leered at her. Emma's face heated. The impertinence of the man! She had never had anyone stare at her that way before.

"Howdy, ma'am. Ya must be Mrs. Hoffman's sister."

Not wishing to be impolite, Emma nodded at the man and turned away.

The man grabbed her arm and turned her back to face him. "No need ta be rude. Just wanted ta get ta know ya." He leered at her again. "Name's Jake, Jake Ballinger."

A shiver of fear raced through Emma at the man's touch on her arm. She pulled herself away, sheltering George from the man as she did. "Excuse me. I need to get my order."

The man's hand was reaching for her again when a voice she recognized as Matthew's boomed across the room. "Keep your grubby hands off of her, Ballinger."

Relief washed through Emma at the sight of Matthew standing in the doorway. She hurried over to him while Mr. McBurney strode over to Ballinger.

Matthew's eyes scanned her from head to foot as Ballinger's had, but instead of lust, his eyes held concern.

"Are you okay?" Matthew asked, frowning.

Matthew had never used such a care-filled or concerned tone before with her. It helped warm her now cold body. "I...I think so. I have never had anyone grab me that way before. I...I'd like to leave now if you're ready." She wanted to smile to reassure Matthew, but she was too shaken at that moment to manage it.

Matthew's arm settled around Emma's shoulder as he led them to the counter. He paid Mrs. McBurney and grabbed the packages. "Let's go home."

Emma and George preceded Matthew out the door and to the wagon. He tossed the packages into the wagon and took George from Emma to help her up into the seat. He gave George a nuzzle on the cheek before handing him back to her and climbing up next to them.

"Thank you, Matthew, for rescuing me. That man frightened me, the way he looked at me..." Emma shivered.

"I'm sorry he was bothering you. He was at the lumber mill when I went over. I didn't realize he had left before I did. He can be a bully," Matthew said.

They both grew quiet. Emma tried to shake the uneasy feeling she had about Ballinger. She wanted to go home and wash where he had touched her. When she looked back over at Matthew, he looked angry. The hard set of his features unsettled her further.

Her churning emotions must have transferred to George. He started to fuss, letting out a loud squall and squirming. She changed his position on her lap and began to sing to try to calm him. Before long, he quieted, and his eyes drifted closed. Emma kept singing because the hymn helped to calm her nerves, too.

The next time she looked over at Matthew, it pleased her to see that his hardness had receded somewhat. She kept singing once they reached the farmstead. She carried the sleeping child into the house where she laid him in his cradle. Emma changed his diaper, pleased that he only stirred long enough to wiggle a bit. When she finished, she covered him and smiled as he burrowed further under the blankets.

Emma didn't miss a beat in her song when she kissed his chubby cheek. She continued to sing as she joined Matthew in the front room. Her song came to an abrupt stop as she drew abreast of him. He was staring out the window, his features set in stone.

Matthew stared out the window, letting his anger at Jake Ballinger overtake him. How dare the man confront Emma when she was alone in the store, let alone touch her? Matthew had about blown his top over that.

A thought niggled its way into Matthew's mind that had him hoping Jake hadn't blabbed to Emma about his predicament with the money he had lost to the mayor. He didn't want Emma to find out about that. He wasn't sure how she would react to it, and he didn't want to find out.

Emma was quiet, so even though she had moved close to share his body heat, it took several minutes for Matthew to realize she had rejoined him. He noticed her when he felt her trembling next to him. He looked down at her pale face. Her eyes were enormous like they had been when Jake accosted her at the store. Inhaling deeply, Matthew let his breath out slowly, trying to put his anger aside.

When he felt calm enough, Matthew pulled Emma close, wrapping his arms around her. She stiffened at first, then she laid her head on his chest as she relaxed against him. One of his hands rubbed up and down her back. The motion soothed his anger as much as he hoped it soothed Emma's fear.

Several minutes went by before Emma pulled away and looked up at him.

"Thank you, Matthew. That man frightened me. I don't know what I would have done if you hadn't come back to the store at that moment."

Matthew shrugged. "I'm glad I was there. Ballinger just better stay clear from now on," he said with a growl. Turning away from Emma, he headed for the door. "I've got to take care of the animals. I'll be back for supper."

It took all the calm he could muster not to slam the door on his way out as his anger started to seethe again. He headed to the barn to take care of the animals.

When Matthew finished his chores, he returned to the big house where the aroma of roast beef made his stomach rumble. He ladled water into the washpan in the kitchen from the bucket he'd brought in for Emma's use. He washed his hands and face in the washpan, getting his hair wet in the process. When he was finished, he dumped the pan outside the back door and returned it to where he had found it on a shelf by the sink.

The table was set for supper. It hit him that they had left town without having a meal there.

Emma greeted him with a shy smile. "Did you get the animals all settled for the night?"

"They're all fine. I was so angry, and you seemed so unsettled that I forgot to stop to eat in town."

"That's all right. I wasn't hungry."

"I'll make up for it next time. How is George doing? I hope Ballinger didn't frighten him."

"George seems fine. He woke up and played while I cooked supper. I fed him and he almost fell asleep while he was eating." She laughed at the memory. "So, I put him to bed."

"That's good. He's already been through enough." Matthew pulled out his chair and took a seat at the table, appreciating the pleasing aroma of the roast wafting from the kitchen.

Emma brought the food to the table and sat down across from Matthew. He led them in Grace then dug into his food with gusto. He had always appreciated Lorette's meals, but Emma's cooking outshone even her sister's.

After they finished eating, Emma cleared the table and brought out a chocolate cake with thick chocolate frosting, and a fresh pot of coffee.

Matthew rubbed his stomach appreciatively. "I didn't think I saved room for dessert but seeing that cake I think I can manage to squeeze in a piece."

Emma laughed as she cut a thick slice of cake and poured a cup of coffee for Matthew. She set both in front of him and proceeded to cut herself a thin piece of the cake.

"That sure is a puny slice of cake you took for yourself." Matthew pointed out with a grunt. He cut into his cake and ate a forkful of the moist cake and the chocolate gooiness that was the frosting.

"Delicious, Emma. Your cakes are the best I've ever eaten. I bet everyone for miles around would flock to buy your cakes if you were to sell them. I feel spoiled to be able to eat them, as well as all the other things you've baked for me." Everything Emma had cooked or baked for him since her arrival had been fantastic.

Emma blushed a bright red at Matthew's compliment, and he realized she was used to living alone and not receiving any praise for her food. He would make sure to let her know how delicious every meal was from now on.

When they finished their dessert and coffee, Emma went to the kitchen to wash the dishes, and Matthew retired to the main room to read the newspaper he had picked up in town. It felt so good and so right.

An article on the bottom of the front page caught his attention. He read it with a feeling of dread.

'Fever and sickness claim two in Valentine.'

Valentine was the next town over. People from Buffalo Springs crossed the border to shop and conduct business in Valentine all the time. Fear raced through him. *Was this the sickness that had killed Michael and his family?* Matthew prayed that it wasn't.

The next evening, Emma watched the emotions crossing Matthew's face as he stood staring out the window. He had the same look he had last night over what happened in town. She found it hard to believe that he was so upset over what that awful Ballinger man had done to her in the store.

Most of the time, Matthew acted as if he just barely tolerated her. His sticking up for her and being so upset about the episode just didn't seem right to Emma. There was something else going on with him and Ballinger. Emma was sure of it.

Crossing the room to Matthew, Emma laid her hand on his shoulder. "Are you alright?"

Matthew spun around a look of surprise on his face. "What?"

Emma's hand slipped from his shoulder at his gruff tone, and she took a step back. "I was just wondering if you are okay?"

"I'm fine. Ballinger just upset me yesterday. He has a way of doing that. But how are you doing today?"

Wrapping her arms around herself to stop the shaking that had started again at the mention of the man's name, Emma took another step back.

"I'm still shaken but I'll be all right after a good night's sleep. I slept poorly last night, so I think I'll turn in. It's been a long day." She turned toward the stairs, hoping Matthew would take the hint and leave. She didn't think she could deal with his mood swings anymore right now.

Matthew took a step toward her and put his hand on her arm to stop her retreat. "Emma..."

Emma shook his hand free and without turning around said, "I'm going to bed, Matthew. It's time for you to go home and do the same."

Once ensconced in her room, Emma collapsed on the bed, the shaking uncontrollable as she thought about the events in town and Matthew's subsequent behavior. She didn't understand any of it and she most definitely did not understand men.

She wished Lorette were there for her to talk things over with. They had shared everything throughout their lives. Her death left an empty spot in Emma's heart that she didn't think would ever heal.

She should visit Maddie, their neighbor. She hadn't seen her since the day she'd arrived at the ranch. Maddie could be a good friend and confidant. Feeling a little less alone in a topsy-turvy world, Emma finally managed to calm down enough to change into her nightclothes and climb into bed.

She would also talk to Matthew about everything tomorrow. His anger frightened her, but he'd been through a lot lately, too. She had to remember that she wasn't the only one grieving right now.

As she lay in bed, Emma couldn't help thinking about what had happened in the store. There was something about that Jake Ballinger

man that made her wary. She hoped she never had another run-in with
him, especially if she was alone.

M atthew stood watching her take the steps one at a time as she
ascended them. *Dagnabbit.* He hadn't meant to frighten her off
with his temper, but he was so upset with Ballinger that he was having
a tough time putting it to rest.

He grabbed his hat from the chair by the door where he'd thrown
it when he'd come by after chores. He pulled the door open. With one
last look toward the staircase, he walked out, slowly closing the door
behind him.

He was never going to get anywhere with Emma if he kept letting
his temper take over. Ballinger would love it if he knew Emma had
thrown him out.

Chapter 7

The next day, Emma hummed as she hung out freshly washed bedding. Who would have thought she would enjoy work she had considered drudgery back home in the city? She smiled as she took in the big black pot full of laundry bubbling over an open fire behind the house.

George cooed and 'talked' to her, making her laugh. She and George were becoming good friends. He loved to play outdoors, but soon there would be too much snow and it would get too cold for him to be outside for very long, if at all. Matthew had told her it was a milder autumn than most.

Emma was glad about the nice weather. She hummed as she hung the bedding up on the line. It was the last load. The clothes were already done and dried.

By the time everything was done drying, dark clouds were scudding toward them.

"Oh, oh, George, looks like playtime is up for the day. A storm is coming." She scooped the toddler up and hurried to the house. He giggled at being jiggled, making her chuckle.

She hoped Matthew would get home from the livestock auction in town before it got too bad, but sometimes he stayed at a sale until the very end.

Matthew had been in a better mood this morning when she saw him. He didn't seem so angry about what had happened the other day in the General Store.

A few hours later, Emma was taking bread out of the oven when she glimpsed a horse and rider approaching from the direction of town. She had hoped it was Maddie, but Maddie would have brought a wagon to accommodate her son.

Emma wanted to visit Maddie today, but she had too much work to do and hoped to make it over to visit her friend the next day. Emma decided that the rider must be Matthew returning earlier than usual from the sale.

As the sky darkened and flakes of snow began to fall, Emma couldn't help but remember the incident in the store and Matthew's reaction to it. She hoped his going to town hadn't turned his mood sour again.

Exhausted from playing outside, George was in his room asleep, so Emma had some time alone. She'd used that time to bake fresh bread and was putting a chocolate cake in the oven.

She smiled as she remembered Matthew's praise the other night for her cakes. She had always been proud of her cooking, but Lorette had always outshone her in everything. It had been Lorette's cooking and baking that everyone had praised.

Pushing that unkind thought away, Emma squinted out the window to see who the rider was, but he had ridden toward the barn and was no longer in sight of that window.

Emma sighed as a prickle of alarm snaked along her skin. She shook it off, attributing it to the gloomy weather that had overtaken the day.

Moments later anxiety forked through her when the front door opened and slammed shut again. *Oh no, Matthew must be in one of his moods.*

The thought had barely cleared Emma's mind when Jake Ballinger strode into the kitchen. Emma froze. She'd never dreamed he would dare stride into her kitchen uninvited.

Backing against the sideboard, Emma held the towel out like a shield. "What are you doing here, Mr. Ballinger?" She hoped her voice sounded more confident than she felt.

Ballinger sneered at her. "I saw your man in town, so I thought I'd come out so we can have a proper visit without his interference." He lunged toward Emma, but she managed to sidestep him.

"You'd better leave. Matthew will be home soon, and he won't appreciate you being here *uninvited*."

"Oh, he won't be here for a while. He's busy trying to scare up some work to make it through the winter and to have seed and livestock feed next spring."

Emma frowned. "Matthew doesn't need to scare up work. He has plenty of money for everything we need," she said, hoping that was true. She had no idea about the condition of Matthew's finances.

Jake sneered again. "He lost everything to the mayor before you arrived. He lost it all to the mayor playing poker in the saloon. Didn't he tell you? He's taken quite a shine to the whisky the bartender has there, too."

The man let out a guffaw. "Why one night, he was so drunk, he couldn't find his way outta the saloon."

Eyes narrowing, Emma asked, "Mr. Ballinger, why are you here and why do feel it necessary to tell me these things? They're none of our business."

"Oh, honey, I think you should know everything about the man yer living with."

Emma backed away as he tried to draw nearer to her. "You just want to cause trouble for Matthew, but why? What do you have against him?" She prayed what the man said was nothing more than his drunken imagination and that Matthew hadn't lost everything they needed to make it through the winter.

Lorette had written to her about the harsh winters and how hard it was some years to have enough money to get them through to spring with money left over to feed the livestock and have seed money that year. She shivered at the thought that Matthew could have endangered them all that way.

Somehow over the last few weeks, Emma had started to have feelings for Matthew, had come to trust him, and had even stopped dreaming about taking George back to Philadelphia with her to live. But if what Ballinger said was true, Emma wasn't sure she would be able to trust Matthew enough to stay here to raise George with him.

Jake's next words brought Emma back to the present situation at hand. This man frightened her more than she had ever been frightened before. She wasn't sure why, but she had a great desire to grab George and flee.

"I think you would make me a fine woman, so I came to take you home with me while Matthew's busy in town."

Slinking away from him toward the parlor and the stairs, Emma prayed that Matthew would return home at any moment to rescue her and George. She had a sinking feeling in her stomach and was afraid things wouldn't end well if Matthew didn't make it back soon.

As soon as she was near the stairway, Emma lifted her skirts, turned, and fled up the stairs, hoping she could outrun the drunk man who was after her.

Seconds later, Ballinger had hold of Emma's foot and was pulling her down the stairs towards him.

With a scream, Emma grabbed for the rail, catching hold of a baluster instead. She stopped herself so suddenly that it jerked both her arm and the leg Ballinger was tugging on. Pain shot through her body.

Struggling to hold onto the bannister, Emma kicked furiously at the man with her free foot. It landed in his face, and he released her foot. She jumped to her feet and fled the rest of the way up the stairs to George's bedroom.

Footsteps on the stairs behind her sent her fleeing into the baby's room. She managed to slam the door shut. She threw the bolt home just as the footsteps pounded across the hallway floorboards to her door.

Ballinger pounded on the door. "Come on now, girl, let me in. Stop playin' hard to get. I know you fell for me the moment you saw me, just like I fell for you."

Shaking all over, Emma glanced down at George. The noise had awakened him, but thankfully he wasn't crying. He stared at her with trust in his big brown eyes.

A fierce protectiveness rose in Emma, and she pulled herself up, forcing the shaking to stop. She prayed that George would stay silent. She didn't think she could deal with the situation if he started to cry. The boy continued to look up at her, confident she would protect him from whatever threat lay beyond the door.

By this point, Ballinger was throwing himself against the door, trying to break it down.

Emma glanced around the room, taking in its contents, hoping that there was something she could use as a weapon. A stack of diapers lay clean on a shelf near the baby's bed and a small box of safety pins to hold them closed.

She spotted a lantern standing on the shelf near the diapers. There was also a small chest that held George's clothing.

Ballinger's body hit the door with a thud. Emma heard wood splintering.

Matthew hated that he had to go into town. He had a bad feeling about leaving Emma and George alone at the farm, but she had refused to come after what had happened the other day.

He was relieved that Emma hadn't wanted to come. It would be easier to search for a job without her and George along. He just had to make things quick, so they weren't left home alone too long.

By that afternoon, Matthew was getting tired of being told there was no work available anywhere in town. He had checked everywhere, even at the lumber mill where he didn't want to work at all. It was dangerous work and something he wasn't used to doing, so normally he wouldn't apply there.

But things were different this time around. He had messed up big time by drinking too much liquor and gambling with the mayor. Now, he had to make it up somehow, but he had no idea how with no work available.

The thought that he might have to travel elsewhere to find work entered his mind, but he pushed it aside. He didn't want to leave Emma and George at home for long periods at a time, if he didn't have to.

He could take them with him but then there would be no one to look after the farm and take care of the animals. Besides, he couldn't push all that work off on Emma when he was the one who had lost the money. He just prayed she wouldn't find out about it before he had a chance to make it all back.

Either one of those scenarios was likely to send her scurrying back to Philadelphia, taking George with her. Matthew didn't want that to happen. He would find a way somehow to earn the money back.

The weather had turned, with a chilly wind blowing from the north now. The large flakes of snow that started to fall spurred Matthew into action. He hurried to the livery and collected his horse. Once he had the horse saddled, he took off as fast as he dared go.

The dark clouds that had overtaken the sky were like a dark omen telling him he needed to get home. He needed to get there now. Spurring the horse to go faster, he squinted to see through the thick blanket of snow that was now falling.

Matthew had noticed Ballinger in town earlier, but he hadn't seen him in quite a while. A tingle raced down his spine. He had not felt such a need to get home since the day he'd heard about Michael and his family being sick.

His thoughts raced back to that day. He'd had that same sick feeling in his stomach that he was experiencing right now.

Please let George and Emma be okay.

By the time the farm came into view, the snow had gathered so much on the road that it was making it hard to see where the road was. At this rate, Matthew would need to get the sleigh out tomorrow.

They'd been lucky so far since the fall had been mild, but it looked as if their luck had run out. This looked to be a mighty storm. He cursed himself for leaving home today. He should have taken heed of the bad feeling in his gut before he'd left. He should have stayed home.

As he turned into the drive leading to the main house, Matthew noticed a horse tied to the hitching post out front. When he got closer, he recognized the horse, Jake Ballinger's. His breath caught in his throat.

Matthew's horse had not completely stopped when Matthew jumped off and raced to the house.

The front door dangled by the top hinge as if it had been broken. Matthew's stomach churned as he raced through the downstairs rooms searching for Emma and George when he heard wood breaking on the upper floor. By the time he made it to the second step, a scream made his blood run cold and his fear turned to burning rage.

Matthew raced the rest of the way up the stairway, taking the stairs two at a time. He sped into George's room and stopped abruptly when he took in the scene before him.

Chapter 8

E mma screamed. She pulled George's clothes chest away from the wall and shoved it against the door. She glanced over at George to ensure he wasn't frightened. He was still looking at her with full trust in his large brown eyes. She'd protect that little boy with her life!

The door shook against the weight of Ballinger's bulk. More wood splintered.

Another scream escaped Emma. Determined, she grabbed the hurricane lamp from the bedside table and moved nearer the door. Her heart pounding in her ears, she flattened against the wall next to the clothes chest. Her hands shook so badly she feared she might drop the lamp.

With one final blow, the wood splintered off its hinges. The door swung open and banged into the low dresser. Ballinger shoved the dresser out of his way and strode into the room, turning his head from side to side.

While his head was turned away from her, Emma gripped the lamp tightly and smashed it over Jake Ballinger's head.

He collapsed to the floor with a groan.

Emma ran to the baby's bed and scooped George up, turning to run out past the unconscious man. She let out a gasp of surprise when Matthew charged through the doorway. He skidded to a stop when he saw Ballinger lying unconscious on the floor.

Holding George, Emma looked at him as tears slid down her cheeks.

Matthew rushed into the room and pulled Emma and George into his arms. "Are you both okay?"

Unable to answer, Emma nodded, snuggling deeper into Matthew's warm embrace. The shaking started again.

Matthew's protective arms tightened around her and George. She laid her head against his shirtfront, letting it soak up her tears. His strong heartbeat sounded in her ears. She needed his strength.

Ballinger moaned, causing Emma to start.

"I don't want to turn you loose, but Ballinger might be coming around. I'd better get him tied up before he regains consciousness and does something stupid," Matthew said as he reluctantly let Emma go and bent over the man.

Emma made a wide berth around them as she took George and headed for the door. She hurried down to the kitchen, unable to stomach the sight of Jake Ballinger any longer.

She had never been so frightened in her life. Not only had she had to protect herself, but she'd had to ensure George's safety also. A sense of pride overtook her as the events played over in her mind. She had managed to knock the man out and save herself and George. Matthew's showing when he did was a godsend.

Heat rushed through Emma when she thought about Matthew holding her and George in his arms and comforting them. It was good to know Matthew could be counted on in times like that.

Ballinger's words about Matthew's gambling away all the money they'd soon need niggled in her memory. Was he lying? If not, that information presented a big problem in more ways than one.

Emma had no patience for a man who imbibed in alcohol and gambled. She would not trust her future and George's with a man like that. It might be best if she packed George up at her first chance and went back to Philadelphia.

Melancholy overtook Emma when she thought about leaving. She had become fond of the farm and enjoyed living out where they had plenty of space instead of being cramped in a tenement house. Perhaps she would go somewhere else and start completely over with George.

All she knew right now was that she was relieved Matthew was home to take care of Ballinger, but she also had a few things to discuss with him. She would find out whether what Ballinger had said was true or whether the man had just been trying to cause trouble for Matthew.

Too shaken up and confused to think clearly, Emma collapsed into the rocking chair with George on her lap.

Moments later, Matthew came down the stairs. "I had a length of rope and got Ballinger tied up." He approached her chair, his eyes roaming over her and George as if making sure for himself that they were both okay.

The warmth of his hand connected with Emma's chin as he turned her face up to his and studied it. "Are you sure you're alright?"

"I'm just shaken up. George is just fine. He was a trooper the whole time."

"I'll fix the door, then I'm going to need to take Ballinger into town to the sheriff. Will you and George be okay here alone until I get back?"

Fear surged through Emma at the thought of being left alone right now but she didn't want Jake Ballinger to remain there. She stiffened her spine and sat up a bit straighter. Summoning all the courage that she could muster, she said, "We'll be fine once that man is gone. I'll have supper waiting for you when you return."

Matthew threw Jake up onto the man's horse and tied him to it so he wouldn't fall off. Once Matthew was seated on his horse, he grabbed the reins from Jake's horse and started toward town.

For some reason, the trip to town seemed to be taking forever. Matthew needed to deliver his prisoner and return to Emma and George. Even though Emma had assured them they would be fine, Matthew would feel better once he was back home with them.

The two men were a few miles outside of town when Ballinger began fighting his bonds and swearing at Matthew. "I'll get you for this Hoffman," he slurred.

Ignoring the threat, Matthew rode on, hoping Ballinger would feel differently once he was sober. Of course, the man was mean-spirited, so that wasn't likely. He'd likely be worse.

If he had to, Matthew would always keep Emma and George with him to keep them safe from Ballinger. That was if Ballinger hadn't blabbed to Emma about his losing all his money to Mayor Hustkins.

Ballinger kept his running dialogue of foul curses the rest of the way into town. He was making such a ruckus that the sheriff heard him and came out of his office to see what was going on. A few shop owners and other people gathered on the street.

"What's goin' on, Matthew?" Sheriff Miller asked.

"I caught Ballinger out at my place trying to accost my sister-in-law," Matthew said. "He's drunk as a skunk and has been making threats."

The sheriff looked up at the drunk man who was finally quiet. "That right, Jake?"

"I ain't done nothin' wrong, sheriff. Hoffman here just has a grudge against me. His woman attacked me. She hit me over the head with the lamp."

The sheriff managed to keep a straight face, although Matthew could see him struggling not to laugh.

"Sounds like you've had a rough night, Jake," the sheriff replied. "How about we get you down off your horse and you can come on in the jail and lie down for a spell."

Sheriff Miller helped Matthew untie Ballinger. They took him into the jail and tossed him onto a cot inside a cell. The sheriff shut the cell door and escorted Matthew back out to the front.

Sitting down, the sheriff leaned back in his chair. "Okay, Matthew, what happened?"

"I told you the truth. Ballinger is lying."

"Okay, okay. Settle down. I'll get you some coffee and you can tell me everything."

In the background, Ballinger was swearing again, but now his curses included the sheriff as well as Matthew.

After telling everything he knew to the sheriff, Matthew sat back in his seat. "Well, that's everything I know."

The sheriff took a sip of his coffee. He set the cup down and looked Matthew in the eye. "I've known you a long time, Matthew. I know you don't lie, but asking these questions is part of my job."

"But..." Matthew said, sensing there was more.

"I still need to have Miss Cantrell come in and tell me what happened in her own words during the time that you weren't present."

"I understand, but she may be too frightened to come into town to talk to you."

The sheriff nodded. "Why don't I just ride out to your place tomorrow? She can tell me everything then. That should make her feel better about having to explain everything to me."

Matthew nodded and picked up his hat which he'd set on the sheriff's desk when he sat down. "I'll be heading home then, and we'll see you tomorrow."

The house was quiet after Matthew left to take Jake Ballinger to the sheriff. Emma fed George some mashed potatoes left over from the night before to tide him over until supper. When he was finished, she sat him down on his blanket to play while she cooked the rest of the meal.

Once George was playing on the floor with his blocks, he made gurgling and squealing noises, dissipating the eerie quietness. Emma knew she was safe since Matthew had taken the threat with him, but she was still nervous being alone with just George after dark.

Emma started humming a hymn while she worked. The noise blended with George's baby noises and helped soothe her frazzled nerves somewhat. *If only Lorette were still alive and I lived here. We'd have a grand time together.*

Sighing, Emma wiped at the tears that escaped when she thought about Lorette. *Oh, Lorette, I wish you were here for me to talk to.*

When the meal was ready, Emma fed George and took him upstairs to get him ready for bed. She didn't feel comfortable laying him in his bed in the room where Jake's attack had taken place. Besides, Matthew was going to need to fix the door, so she took George back downstairs and laid him on his blanket on the floor near the warmth of the fire.

George's eyes soon fluttered closed, and he slipped into sleep. Emma stood watching him, grateful she had the chance to know him and be a part of his upbringing.

The sound of a horse galloping up the drive brought Emma out of her reverie with a start. The sound of horse beats sent a shiver through her. That was how the whole horrible afternoon had started.

Her palms grew sweaty as she peered out the front window in dread. She let out a sigh of relief when she recognized Matthew's silhouette and his horse heading to the barn. She hurried to the kitchen to put the food on the table.

Emma met Matthew at the door when he entered. She wrung her hands as she looked at him, trying to keep her voice steady. "Did everything go all right?"

Matthew nodded. "I got Ballinger to the sheriff, and he threw him in a cell. I explained what happened, but the sheriff said he needed to hear your side of the story."

Shivering, Emma shook her head. "I don't know if I can make a trip to town so soon."

"That's okay. The sheriff said he'd be out tomorrow to talk to you." Matthew approached Emma and put a hand on each shoulder as he looked her in the eye.

"I'll be right here. I'm going to stick close to the house from now on. I don't need to make a trip into town for a while and when I do, you and George can come with me, or I can drop you off to visit Maddie while I go."

"Thank you, Matthew. That makes me feel better. I'm afraid I may have a hard time for a while being at the ranch alone."

Matthew's arms encircled Emma, pulling her close against his chest. "I'm sorry you had to go through that."

Sighing, Emma relaxed against him, enjoying the warmth of his body and the safety she felt in his arms. After a few minutes, she pulled away. "I've got supper on the table."

Once they sat down and said Grace, Matthew dug into his food with his usual gusto. Emma still felt queasy after Ballinger's attack and picked at her food, taking a small bite here and there.

Eating a forkful of potatoes and gravy, Matthew looked over at her. "You should eat more. You don't eat enough for a bird."

"I'm afraid I don't have much of an appetite this evening," Emma said. Not only was the frightening episode with Jake Ballinger playing over and over in her head, but she was also still worried about what Ballinger had said about Matthew.

Too exhausted and shaken to do anything about it tonight, she vowed she would speak with Matthew about it tomorrow. After she knew the truth, she could decide what she and George would do.

Chapter 9

Matthew was worried about Emma. She usually had a robust appetite, but tonight she was barely picking at her food. He hoped she would be all right after Ballinger's attack.

After supper, Matthew hung around, not sure he wanted to leave Emma and George alone even though he knew the sheriff held Ballinger in jail. His protective instincts had risen when he'd come home to find Ballinger here and they hadn't settled down yet.

He turned to Emma to tell her his thoughts when she approached him.

"Matthew, I know Jake Ballinger is in jail, but I'm not sure I want George and me to be alone tonight." Emma blushed bright red. "Would you mind staying here? You could sleep in one of the extra rooms."

Relief surged through Matthew. Now, he didn't need to ask Emma about staying to keep an eye on them.

Matthew nodded. "Of course. I've got to take care of the animals, but then I'll be back."

Not sure if he could stand to sleep in one of Michael's kids' rooms so soon after their deaths, he said, "I can just grab a blanket and sleep on the couch. That way I'm down here, closer to the door."

"Thank you, Matthew. I'll get the bedding and make up the couch for you."

Matthew nodded and headed toward the door. "I'll be back as quick as I can."

Once he was outside, Matthew flew through the nightly chores and hurried back inside to find the lamp in the front room glowing. He glanced over at the couch and found it already made up with blankets and a feather pillow. Emma was nowhere in sight.

Going in search of her he found the rest of the house to be dark, including the upstairs. Emma must have gone to bed.

Too wound up to sleep, Matthew paced about the front room until he felt sleepy enough to retire.

T he next morning, Matthew rose before Emma did. He stirred the fire in the stove and started the coffee. Then he went out to take care of the animals for the morning and collect the eggs.

When he returned, Emma was in the kitchen frying bacon, and George was waiting patiently for his oatmeal.

Matthew gave George a good morning kiss, resisting the urge to take Emma in his arms and kiss her good morning. Instead, he grabbed a cup and poured himself some coffee.

"It's chilly out today. Looks like more snow's coming," Matthew said before taking a careful sip of the hot coffee.

Emma nodded. "The sky sure is gray." She spooned oatmeal into a bowl for George.

Matthew reached out, taking the bowl from her. "I'll feed George today."

With another nod, Emma turned back to the stove.

Sitting down next to George, Matthew scooped up a spoonful of oatmeal, blowing on it to cool it before offering it to George. George leaned forward and gobbled up the cereal with a grin.

A deep laugh escaped Matthew. He scooped up another spoon of the gooey oatmeal and held it out, away from George's mouth. He made a galloping motion as he moved the spoon closer to the baby's mouth. "Open the gate, here comes the stage."

Giggling, George opened his mouth on cue. Matthew galloped the spoon inside, saying, "Whoa."

George giggled again. Emma smiled at Matthew and the baby. Love for the two of them welled up in Matthew, surprising him that it included Emma. *I'm not in love with Emma, am I?*

The thought hit Matthew like a bolt of lightning striking a lone tree on the prairie. *What? No, I can't possibly be in love with her. How can that be? How can it have happened?*

Absorbed in his newfound knowledge, it took several moments before he realized Emma had brought all the food to the table and was speaking to him. He looked over at her, stunned.

His heart, which had soared at the thought of loving Emma, dove down to his stomach, and settled there like a lump when Emma repeated words that froze his blood.

Emma eyed Matthew, her anger building inside her when she realized he had no idea what she had just said to him. Her voice cold and impatient, she said, "I have some things I need to discuss with you as soon as we've finished eating and I put George down to play."

The silly grin on Matthew's face became a frown.

"What..." He cleared his throat. "What do you need to talk to me about?"

The forkful of eggs on the way to her mouth paused in midair. She eyed him again, expression serious. "We'll discuss it after breakfast."

Matthew sat back. Puzzlement and defeat clouded his expression.

"You better eat your food before it grows cold," Emma said, waving her empty fork from his plate to his mouth.

Sitting forward, Matthew picked up his fork and took a bite of eggs.

Emma could tell he was worried about conversing with her after their meal because he didn't compliment the food as he usually did after taking his first bite of any meal.

Well, that worried look on your face doesn't bode well. Emma shifted in her seat, worried now herself. If he was worried, then he must be afraid Ballinger had told her something. *What if he really did drink and gamble away all the farm money? I was so sure he wouldn't have done such a thing.*

Her appetite gone, Emma pushed her plate away and scooped George up from the seat he was propped up in. George rubbed his eyes. Sleep was overtaking him.

"Last night must have tuckered George out more than I realized. I think I'd better put him down for a nap."

George gave a giant yawn. Matthew sighed as he watched the baby. "I'll be right here," he said, resignation clear in his voice.

Upstairs in her bedroom, Emma worked on calming her roiling emotions while she changed George. She had moved George's furniture and his cradle into her room the previous night before putting George to bed. Once George was fresh and dry, she laid him in his cradle and sang a hymn in a low voice.

George was asleep long before Emma's anger ebbed. She continued singing until she felt calm enough to confront Matthew. Then she made her way back downstairs to join him.

Matthew's face held an apprehensive expression as Emma approached him. "Matthew, I have something important to discuss with you." At his nod, she continued, "I..." Unsure how to broach the subject, she paused.

"Go on," Matthew urged.

"Well, this is difficult for me to bring up considering it came from that awful man, Jake Ballinger," Emma said. She noted that Matthew paled at the mention of the man's name. Her stomach sank. She plunged on. "He said that you frequent the saloon in town and that you gambled away all the money you had for the farm. Is that true?"

Matthew raised his head. His eyes met Emma's as he scrunched his hat in his hands. "Yes, that is true."

Shock reverberated through Emma. She had so wanted to believe that Matthew would not do such a thing, but he had. She felt as if her stomach sank to her knees. She was unable to reply for several moments as her thoughts swirled in her mind.

Eventually, she said in a whisper, "How could you do such a thing?"

"I...I...," Matthew began.

Emma interrupted, "I don't want to hear any lies or excuses, Matthew. You gambled away George's future. How could you do that?"

Matthew paled even more.

Emma's words made Matthew sound so irresponsible. He felt the size of an acorn when she said them out loud. He couldn't quite meet her eyes. He hated to see the disappointment in them.

"I don't have an excuse for what I did. It was careless and irresponsible just as you said," Matthew muttered. He looked up in time to see Emma's face turn from furious red to pale disbelief. He was in trouble.

"How could you?" Emma's words were barely a whisper.

"In my defense, I haven't set foot in the saloon since your arrival," Matthew said, his voice weak.

Emma swung her dazed gaze to his face, locking eyes with him. "Is that supposed to make me feel better? How could you do such a thing? What about George? What about his future?"

The shame of his actions and Emma's dressing down had Matthew relating to how Michael must have felt the time or two that Lorette had done the same thing when Michael had done something wrong. The only thing different was the fact that what Matthew had done was so much worse than anything Michael had ever done.

"I wasn't thinking at the time about George or about our future or anything else. I was simply grieving over my brother and his family."

It took several moments for Emma to respond. When she did, her voice was somewhat calmer. "I can understand your grieving, but to gamble away your future? That I cannot understand. What do you plan on doing about it? How are you planning to come up with enough money to buy seeds to plant in the spring?"

"I've been searching in town for work, but there's nothing available right now," Matthew admitted.

The furious look returned to Emma's face. It deepened to a shade of crimson. "Well, that's not going to help much, is it?" She bunched her hands into fists at her sides. "I just do not understand it or you. I'm just not sure what to do about this situation. It's obvious that George needs someone more responsible to raise him."

A lump that felt like a large rock settled in the pit of Matthew's stomach. Now, he'd done it. Emma was sure to take George and head back East to raise him on her own. Matthew would likely never see either of them again. His palms grew sweaty. He rubbed them up and down on his pant legs, unsure how to respond to Emma's tirade.

As Emma's anger built, she began pacing back and forth in front of the dining table and wringing her hands. Matthew watched in misery as he thought about the good times he had enjoyed with Emma and George in the weeks since she had arrived.

That was all over now, as well as the fabulous meals that Emma fixed for him. He was going to end up totally alone after losing George to Emma. His heart squeezed. He couldn't lose George or Emma. They were both too dear to him. He had to come up with a way to fix this mess.

He had stopped paying attention to Emma's ranting while he worried over his situation, but her next words speared him.

"I just can't deal with this or you anymore right now. I'd like you to leave, please, Matthew."

Matthew jerked his head up and met Emma's angry gaze.

"I need some time alone to think about this and decide what I need to do for George's future and mine," Emma said when Matthew made no move to leave.

He rose slowly to his feet and retrieved his hat from the chair where he'd thrown it when he arrived. With his heart as heavy as his steps, Matthew turned and left the ranch house, closing the door firmly behind him.

The next morning, the ranch house was locked up tight when Matthew arrived to drop off the fresh milk and eggs with the hopes of being able to join George and Emma for breakfast as he had been doing since Emma's arrival. His hopes and his heart sank.

There was movement inside the house, so he knew Emma was up and about, but it was obvious she didn't want his company today. He left the milk can and the basket of eggs on the porch by the door. After giving a good rap on the door, he turned and headed back to the barn.

Chapter 10

Emma could hear Matthew outside the door, but she was still too furious to even see him, yet. Breakfast that morning was lonely without Matthew, but Emma pushed those feelings aside. It would be just her and George from here on out.

After eating and cleaning up the mess in the kitchen, she carried George upstairs. She took out her travel case and packed her few belongings in it. She carefully added George's things and closed the case.

Now, she was packed and ready to go. She just had to decide where they were going. She didn't have much money, just what she had left from selling the extra milk and eggs to the grocer each week since her arrival at the farm.

Sadness engulfed Emma as she thought about leaving the farm. It was the last link she had to Lorette and her family. Though she had hated it here at first, she had grown to love it as Lorette had. It didn't seem right to take George away from his birthright. She chewed her bottom lip with her teeth as she tried to work out her dilemma.

The rest of the day, she scrubbed the house to ensure it was good and clean before she and George left. While she worked, she continued to worry about whether she should be taking George away from here, and if so, where they should go. By the time suppertime came she was so exhausted she didn't feel like cooking much. It was just her and George anyway. No need for a big fancy meal.

She settled on scrambled eggs with homemade bread slathered in fresh-made butter. Her stomach was unsettled at the thought of leaving Buffalo Springs. She picked at her food, eating just enough to curb her slight hunger so she wouldn't be sick later.

The food did little to settle her grumbling stomach or her roiling emotions. As soon as she finished cleaning the kitchen, she took George upstairs for bed. Once she had him changed and laid down for the night, she changed into her nightclothes and lay down on her own bed.

Emma awoke early the next morning, feeling more refreshed after a good night's sleep, but still unsure about what she and George should do. After a quick breakfast of oatmeal, Emma dressed herself and George in warm clothes and headed to the barn.

The sun was just starting to rise over the horizon. The first light of dawn was weak and streaked with pink and orange.

On a normal morning, Emma would stop to enjoy the beautiful sky and welcome the new day, but today she didn't take time to enjoy the view. Inside the barn, she readied the team of horses and then hooked them to the wagon as Matthew had taught her.

Since she still didn't know what she should do about her situation, she decided that a trip to her neighbor's farm for a visit was in order. She needed some advice and guidance from Maddie.

Once the wagon was ready, she loaded George in his basket onto the seat and then climbed up beside him. Taking up the reins, she clucked to the horses and headed out of the barn and up the driveway to the road.

The trip to Maddie's didn't take long but the drive in the crisp morning air helped clear Emma's head. She had come up with an idea about how she could make a living for herself and George wherever they ended up. The muscles in her shoulders relaxed somewhat after that and she enjoyed the rest of the journey.

Maddie was out doing chores in the barn when Emma arrived. She welcomed Emma as if they were old friends. After getting George out of the wagon, Emma helped Maddie finish her chores. Then they went into the house together.

After the two women had set the little ones down on a blanket on the floor to play with some blocks of wood, Maddie put a dented kettle on her stove and waved for Emma to take a seat at the table. Emma complied and looked at Maddie.

"I need some advice, Maddie. I don't know what to do," Emma confessed.

Maddie placed tea leaves in a tea ball and put it into a chipped teapot. She poured hot water in the teapot to steep before joining Emma at the table. She placed her hand over Emma's which rested on the table. "Tell me what's going on. I'll help in any way I can."

Emma related the whole sordid story to Maddie about Jake's unwanted visit, his revelations about Matthew, and Matthew's guilt.

"My first instinct is to take George and run, but there's nothing left for me in Philadelphia. If we don't stay here in Buffalo Springs, then I don't know where to go," Emma finished as her voice broke and tears glistened in her eyes.

Maddie patted Emma on the back as she stood to retrieve the teapot. "Oh honey, you've got it bad, haven't you?"

Emma raised her eyes to Maddie. "What do you mean?"

Smiling, Maddie poured two cups of tea and handed one to Emma as she rejoined her at the table. "You've fallen in love with Matthew. It seems to me you need to take your love for him into consideration when you make your decision about what to do."

Denial was on Emma's lips, but she said nothing when Maddie held up a hand to silence her.

"Don't bother denying it. I can see it in your eyes and hear it in your voice when you speak of him."

"But how can I love him after what he did?" Deep down Emma knew Maddie was right...she had fallen in love with Matthew, but she didn't want to acknowledge that just yet, not even to herself.

"How can you not be in love with him after his gallant rescue from that no-good Jake Ballinger?" Maddie asked with a grin.

Emma chewed on her bottom lip but didn't have a reply to that question.

"Seriously, Emma, I've known Matthew my whole life. I grew up with him and Michael. They've always been like brothers to me." Maddie paused to take a sip of her tea.

"Believe me, Matthew's drinking and gambling was his reaction to Michael's death. He is not usually a drinker or a gambler. He and Michael were so close that I think he just didn't know how to react to his sudden loss. I do know that he will find a way to set things right and have the money he needs come spring."

Her mind whirling with doubts, Emma asked, "But how can you be so sure?"

"Because I know him. If you really love him, you'll find a way to help him."

Maddie wasn't much older than Emma, but she was wise beyond her years. Her words about Matthew played over and over in Emma's mind on the trip home. She went slowly so she had time to mull over everything Maddie had told her.

Emma had never been in love before, but she knew what Maddie said was true. She was in love with Matthew and needed to stick by him and help him figure things out. It wouldn't be fair to take George away from Matthew or for George to lose Matthew. The two of them had suffered as much loss recently or more than Emma had.

Still, Emma wasn't ready to face Matthew yet. As soon as she reached the farm, she hurriedly unhitched the horses. As soon as she had rubbed them down, she refilled their food bags and water trough. She escaped into the house before she had a chance to run into Matthew.

It was about dark and past George's suppertime, so Emma fixed them a quick meal. After they ate and she cleaned the kitchen, Emma took George upstairs and got him ready for bed. Once she laid him down in his bed, she changed into her nightgown and lay on her bed.

Lying on her side, Emma stared over at George. He was exhausted after their visit with Maddie, so he was asleep almost as soon as Emma put him in his bed. She was exhausted, but sleep eluded her as she worried things over.

The next morning when Emma awoke, the sky was dark, and the threat of snow hung in the air. Emma still wasn't ready to face Matthew, so she stayed indoors and spent the day playing with George and mulling things over.

The snow started to fall around midmorning and turned into a full-blown blizzard by afternoon. The wind howling through the trees that surrounded the house frightened Emma. She cuddled on the sofa with George and watched the storm as it raged outside the window. She was lucky Matthew had stacked plenty of firewood each day when he came by to help her.

Chapter 11

Exhausted, Matthew lay in the dark, a small smile on his lips. He had come up with a way to make back the money he had lost to the mayor. For the past week, he'd rounded up a herd of wild horses. He had them in the pen near the barn so he could saddle-break them and train them for herding and rounding up cattle.

Farmers and ranchers in the area were always in need of a good horse. He would have them trained by spring when he would need the money for seeds to plant. Meanwhile, he had a few steers to sell this next month, so he'd have enough money to buy feed for the rest of the livestock to make it through the winter in case it was a harsh one.

It felt good to have come up with a plan to fix the mess he'd made. He couldn't wait to tell Emma, but she was still avoiding him and had spent most of the week with Maddie. Emma's friend had been the one to take Emma into town to give the sheriff the details of Jake Ballinger's attack on her. They'd gone into town one other day that week to do their shopping.

Matthew couldn't deny the concern that maybe Emma had taken that opportunity to buy her and George a ticket back to Philadelphia. His smile disappeared when he thought about it. He'd missed Emma and George terribly this past week, but he was grateful he had finally come up with his plan about the horses.

The work of tracking the horses and then catching them and bringing them back had been a good way to keep him from thinking about Emma and George constantly. It also helped to make him so tired by nightfall that he usually fell right to sleep once his head hit the pillow.

For some reason he was having trouble getting to sleep tonight. He blamed it on his excitement after making it home with his small bunch of horses he had culled from the larger herd but deep down he knew he was lying to himself. He just missed Emma and George.

He and Emma had gotten to know each other well over the past few months since she came. She had told him stories about the city and about the children she had worked with, the good as well as the bad ones.

She had made him laugh with stories about the brats from her last job so comically he had choked on his meal twice that afternoon.

Matthew had learned a lot about Emma during those talks. He had listened to her talk about the cramped and leaky room she had lived in for years with glowing affection and had listened to her speak about the things she had had to do to keep the kids she looked after excited and entertained.

They also talked about Michael and Lorette. Emma had told him all about her and Lorette as they grew up and how they struggled after their parents were killed in a carriage accident. His heart hurt for them, and he had yearned to ease the pain it was clear Emma still carried from their deaths.

When Emma had explained about her aversion to homesteading, he'd realized it did not make her weak. There was truly hardship everywhere, and just as he had felt terrible when people criticized his choices, he should have accorded Emma the same favor by not criticizing hers, either.

It turned out that Emma was very funny and interesting. She was a lot like Lorette in many ways, including being hardworking like Lorette had been.

The image of Emma's smiling face popped into his head. She was equally as beautiful as she was smart. He had noted her beauty before that night, but as she told him story after story, her hands motioning in the air, her eyes expressive, he hadn't been able to tear his eyes away from her.

Her face had glowed somehow, glowed with happiness and more beauty when she was in storytelling mode. Then she laughed at a silly joke he had made, and his heart had skipped a beat.

Matthew could not understand where all those feelings were coming from. He had not felt anything like it ever since he had broken up with Hannah years ago. And it was tragic timing. His brother and her sister had just been laid to rest a few months earlier, and he was already having missed heartbeats for her.

The feelings had been mutual. He was sure of it. He had caught her staring at him more than once though she had quickly averted her eyes once he had caught her staring.

At that moment Matthew had realized Emma was everything he had prayed for in a wife, but he knew it would never work. Emma was Lorette's sister. Emma loved the city too much, and he was not ready for that emotional roundabout again.

But then the whole episode with Ballinger happened. Emma had clung to Matthew when he found her that day. His hopes had soared until Emma let him know that she had found out about his drinking and gambling binge. Now, she wasn't speaking to him, was avoiding him, in fact.

As Matthew lay in the dark thinking, he realized that if it came down to only one person taking care of George, the child would be far better with Emma than he would ever be with him. Emma would have all the patience, love, and affection a child needed. And she would give it to him in the right doses. Nothing was ever going to happen to George as long as he was in Emma's care.

Banging on his door brought Matthew out of his morose thoughts. He sprang up at once and pulled on his pants. He was fastening his pants when the banging sounded again.

It had been snowing for the past few hours. Matthew couldn't imagine who would be pounding on his door at this time, especially on a night like this. Matthew skipped steps as he bounded down the stairway.

"Matthew?" Emma's frightened voice could barely be heard above the raging of the storm.

He swung the door open to find Emma bundled in a cloak and covered in snow.

"Emma! What is it? What's wrong?" It had to be something bad for her to be out in this storm to seek him out.

"It's George. He's burning hot!" Emma undid her cloak to reveal George wrapped in blankets and strapped to Emma's chest with strips of flannel.

As soon as Emma revealed George bundled under her cloak, Matthew rushed outside to hitch the team to the sleigh while Emma and George got warm by the stove. Once the sleigh was ready, Matthew bundled the two into the it and covered them with a carpet before taking off for town.

Once in town, they went directly to the doctor's house. Matthew didn't hesitate in the least to wake the doctor from a sound sleep.

The grizzly old doctor admitted them to his office. He took George from Emma's arms and headed to the exam room with Matthew following behind as he explained why they were there.

The doctor shooed Matthew out of the exam room and told him to shut the door behind him.

Matthew trudged out of the doctor's small exam room to find Emma standing by the window, shaking so badly that she was vibrating like a leaf in the breeze.

"What did the doctor say?" Emma turned to Matthew as soon as the doctor shut the exam room door.

"Nothing yet. He's still examining George," Matthew said as he walked toward her.

When Emma staggered, Matthew grabbed her before she fell against the window.

"You need to relax. Sit down, at least." Matthew steered her to one of the chairs.

Emma collapsed into the chair. She had struggled through the storm with George to Matthew's house and she looked exhausted. Worry lines creased her face.

Emma lifted her face to his. "What if...?"

"Don't think like that. He will recover and be fine," Matthew assured her.

Emma's eyes were like saucers as fear overtook her. She looked fragile as if she could break at any moment.

Matthew rubbed her tense shoulders absently.

"He's all I have from her..." Emma whispered. Tears made her voice tremble.

Pain sliced through Matthew's heart. George was all he had from Michael.

Matthew pulled her up against his chest, enveloping her in his arms.

Emma clung to him, her tears causing a wet spot on his shirt.

"George will be fine," Matthew whispered against her soft hair, but the tears he was trying to hide rolled silently down his cheeks.

The doctor cleared his throat making Emma and Matthew spring apart.

"George is a mighty sick little tyke. There's no way for me to tell if he has the fever that killed his parents, but I think he should be okay...if he makes it through the night."

Emma gasped.

Matthew took her hand and gave it a gentle squeeze.

The doctor peered out the front window. "That storm is mighty fierce. I want George to stay here tonight so I can keep an eye on him. I don't think you two ought to go back out in that storm tonight, anyway."

Matthew shuffled his feet. He couldn't afford the cost of a room at the hotel.

"I have a few cots and plenty of blankets. We can set something up for you two to get some sleep," the doctor said.

"Can we see him?" Emma asked.

"Of course. You two go on in and see him while I get beds ready," the doctor answered. "You both look like you're going to collapse at any second."

By the next morning, George's fever had broken, and he was looking perkier. The storm let up by midafternoon, so the doctor said they could take George home. They wrapped George in his blankets and Emma strapped him to her chest before bundling him under her cloak as she had the previous night.

Matthew went out to hitch the team to the sleigh. He returned and helped Emma outside and up on the wagon seat.

Once she was seated, Emma adjusted George in her cloak and ensured he had an air hole to breathe through as Matthew climbed aboard and set off. The snow was deep, but the sleigh cut through it easily, so they made good time back to the farm.

When Matthew pulled up in front of the door to the big house, Emma started to get off. Matthew reached out to stop her. "We need to talk."

Emma sighed. She was exhausted. She had been so worried about George, she had hardly slept the previous night. She wanted nothing more than to take George up to bed and join him there. Instead, she said, "Come inside. We can talk there."

Inside, Matthew went to the kitchen to start coffee while Emma took George upstairs to lay him down.

She knew there was a lot they needed to talk about, but she already felt emotionally drained.

She looked down at George who was fast asleep in his swaddling. Dreading the talk with Matthew, Emma took her time changing George and then sang to the sleeping boy. The hymn gave her the strength to go down and face Matthew.

When she trudged into the kitchen, Matthew helped her to a seat at the table and then handed her a cup of fresh hot coffee.

Emma wrapped her hands around the hot cup to warm them as Matthew moved to get his coffee from the counter behind her.

"I think you should take George," Matthew said.

Emma swiveled around in shock. That was the last thing she had expected him to say. "What?"

"Take George," he repeated. "You will be a better and more doting parent than I would be."

"What happened to homesteading being the best life?" Emma smiled.

Matthew let out a snort. "We both know it isn't, and we both know there are dangers..."

"There are dangers in the city," Emma countered.

Yes, but you are better with him and..."

"Well, I'm not taking him."

Stunned, Matthew raised his eyes to hers. "What?"

"I planned to at first, but this is his home. This is his life. I can't just tear him away from it. Besides, the country is a much better place to raise a kid than the city is."

"I can't take care of him that way, Emma. I love him so much, but I can't do..."

"I didn't say I was leaving, either," Emma pointed out. "I thought it over and decided it's best if I stay. I can bake and sell cakes to make money to help get the funds we need for the farm."

Matthew laughed. "And I came up with the idea of catching wild horses to train and sell. I spent this past week catching some. As soon as the weather clears up, I'll start breaking them."

Emma laughed too. "That's terrific. I can't wait to see them."

"What made you change your mind about staying?" Matthew asked.

"I'm beginning to understand my sister's love for this land. I thought it was a harsh place, but it has made me realize and respect nature. I'm amazed at how this place always seems to replenish what is lost..." She turned to Matthew and stuttered to a stop at the emotion she saw in his eyes as he looked at her.

"We..." she whispered. "We are not in a tussle with the land. We are its partners, working to help replenish it. Besides, George needs you, too. There are so many things I wouldn't be able to get done or teach him without you."

"You don't have to." Matthew's voice sounded husky with emotion.

Emma could not move or look away. Her heart fluttered wildly in her chest as she searched the brown depths of his eyes. "What do you mean?" she asked in a whisper.

"Marry me, Emma."

Tears flowed down Emma's face as she threw her arms around Matthew and their lips met.

Epilogue

Emma looked across at Matthew staring down at their newborn daughter asleep in her arms. Love for her husband swelled in Emma's heart.

The two had married as soon as George recovered from his illness. Emma couldn't believe that was almost two years ago now. She also couldn't believe she had ever wanted to leave this beautiful land and go back to the city. She would never leave this land or her family.

"You're as beautiful as your mother," Matthew said to the baby.

Emma reached over and squeezed his hand. Her heart overflowed with love for him and her family. She must be the luckiest woman alive.

George could be heard padding down the hall toward their bedroom, Matthew jumped up to waylay the toddler to keep him from barreling through the door and climbing onto the bed like he usually did.

The child's eyes were huge with wonder when he stared at the newest member of their family.

Emma laughed with happiness. She had found her new life, and it was better than she'd ever anticipated.

Thank you for reading A New Life for Emma!

CONNECT WITH THE AUTHOR/PUBLISHER:

Check out the Kayler Rose Publishing website and join our newsletter email list!

https://kaylerrosepublishing.com/

If you liked *A New Life for Emma,* by Taylor Aspen, you might be interested in reading *A Mail-Order Bride for the Shopkeeper,* by Rhiana Rhiley, both published by Kayler Rose Publishing, LLC! You can find more information and a link to retailers at https://kaylerrosepublishing.com/

About the Author

Taylor Aspen writes historical romance. This is her first published historical romance book.

Taylor lives in Colorado. She loves romance and history, so combined the two with her love of writing to write historical romances.

You can find more information about Taylor Aspen on the Kayler Rose Publishing website listed below.

Read more at https://kaylerrosepublishing.com/.